A Subtle Armageddon

A Subtle Armageddon

Charles Martin Cosgriff

Writers Club Press
San Jose New York Lincoln Shanghai

A Subtle Armageddon

Writers Club Press
an imprint of iUniverse, Inc.

For information address:
iUniverse, Inc.
5220 S. 16th St., Suite 200
Lincoln, NE 68512
www.iuniverse.com

ISBN: 0-595-20304-3

Printed in the United States of America

PROLOGUE

Deep in the bowels of a long forgotten place a female form lay, naked and unmoving. It appeared unaware of its surroundings, the eyes staring blankly at the soothing whiteness of the ceiling above. Likewise the figure was unaware of the procedure just completed, the sole procedure for which she had been created. She remained motionless for several moments, as the light which emanated from above verified the success of the action. Once informed that all was as it should be the woman rose and left the room.

For months this biological necessity roamed the corridors and rooms of the building she was in, eating and sleeping as need be, and having regular checkups. Things were no different than before in that respect. It was never bothered that she should be clothed; she never went outdoors, and the internal atmosphere kept her warm and comfortable. Further, clothing was basically just a sign of one's station in life. This woman's rank did not matter.

There were, for now, no men. Neither were there other women, and there could be no more after her. This woman was the means to the end she carried, beyond which there was nothing. It had taken time, much time, as the process went on, fertilizations and then instant destructions as the products failed to meet the standards set. Finally the right combination was hit upon, and promptly put in storage until a female body had matured.

The day came that the woman was lying on a table in the room where the original procedure had taken place. The swelling in her abdomen was scanned and deemed fit. The woman was oblivious to the scanning, and to the low mechanical whirring and humming going on around her. She was in no pain, as had been proscribed. The woman lay without moving or making any sound, until her eyes gently closed to the eternal sleep.

The mechanical noises went on for a few minutes longer. Then came a quiet which might have been forever. There was the briefest impulse of failure, that perhaps the time had not been right, or the carrier too weak to have been effective with the task. Finally the silence was broken by the shrill screams and harsh coughs of the male infant.

CHAPTER ONE

It was one of the oddest sensations the man had ever known. He was walking a straight line through psychedelic patterns which scurried around him. Brilliance flashed and faded, sometimes red, sometimes blue or green. Complete silence accompanied the colors. They moved at tremendous speeds in all directions, passing even overhead and underfoot. Then the colors began to push through his body. One would race up to him, slow nearly to a stop as if observing its prey, then methodically surround and penetrate the man as he walked on. Each color occupied him for a few moments and then moved out, dancing about behind the man as they moved farther along. They acted as though someone else were coming.

Many of the colors moved through him, maybe two dozen, maybe three. Each left some bit of itself within him, although the man could not perceive exactly what those bits might be. They were more than color. They ingrained themselves into his being, becoming fully part of him, so subtly that it was not apparent a new man had been produced.

And then he was falling. Downward he plummeted, increasing in speed all along. He soon reached the point where he could go no faster, before finally hitting bottom with a shattering thud. A tremor ran through his body, and in the instant after he woke the man heard the leaves beneath him rustle.

To this he offered no response. Asleep one minute, he was simply awake the next. The forest around him was quiet, while the morning sun steadily lit the sky. The man had been wandering these woods for several days now, and happened last night to sleep at the edge of a small clearing. He had fallen asleep precisely when fatigue dictated.

The man sat up, looking here and there but not comprehending his surroundings. Realizing, or rather being brought to realize, that he needed nourishment, the man reached into a back pocket and pulled out a blue stick and ate it. Likewise he produced a yellow tablet, deftly popping it into his mouth. The day's first meal was typically unexciting. The same breakfast he'd had for years.

Suddenly the man rose: it was something more profound than merely standing up. In one swift, graceful movement he was off the ground and perfectly erect. He stood as a statue, solid and formidable, as if ready to meet any challenge. Muscular, yes, but his muscles failed to dominate his appearance. His skin was golden, his hair a striking blond, his head square-jawed with deep set eyes. The Europeans had managed to dominate the world after all.

He wasn't handsome yet he was good looking. Perfectly good look-ing, as though a reasonably appealing image had been purified. The man's body was proportioned remarkably well. The arms precisely matched the torso, as did the legs match both, and so forth. No single feature was out of size to another. The exactness of fit so complemented the totality of the man that every body part, every area was emphasized. Everything stood out, which had the effect of balance. Each was seen as each should be: a functional part of a human organism, each to its own form, with their own particular duties.

The man began walking forward. At first one would have the impres-sion he did so on purpose. This was far from the case. The man had no clear idea of what he was doing or where he was going. His direction was not affected by free will but was merely the way he went. The illu-sion of purpose was the result of an inborn random decisiveness, so finely tuned that a casual observer would be easily fooled. If the man had no specific instructions he simply went in the direction he happened to turn.

For quite a long time the man walked, several hours as we would know it. The sun rose majestically in the sky to his right. Distant mountains to his left grew out of a shadowy greyness into a fine colorful panorama. Browns, whites, and greens accented the mountain ridge. Straight ahead the man still walked, past giant trees which had survived the test of time. He marched through light brush, grazing the unnoticed wildflowers and bending a few stems along the way. His feet crunched upon the ground, sending a firm message as to who was its lord. Yet as the man pressed on he never once took particular notice of where he was or what was around him.

The man stopped abruptly. Something had indicated it was time for lunch. He sat down on the grass and produced a pill and a stick similar to those which had made up his breakfast. Once they were consumed he took out a white pill and ate it. It was a calcium supplement. At least the mid-day meal offered him a change of pace.

With the end of lunch came a problem. The man was notified that his food supply had dropped below a recommended level. He had seven days worth left, eight considered the minimum safe reserve. He would have to visit a food station for resupply. The man was a relatively short distance from one, yet he didn't really 'know' that. Strictly on his own he would within reason never find it. But his internal controls would care for him.

The patch of grass which had made for his lunch table fell quickly and certainly behind the man. His measured stride amounted to a confident haste, more than a stroll but less than a racer's pace. Not to be lost on the onlooker was the pleasure of seeing the man's body move. Its gracefulness was alive, sensual. Body parts not only fit perfectly but worked perfectly together. A step consisted of a single fluid motion. There was no jerking or stuttering as each step became the next. The repetitive joy in observation could lull a man to sleep.

The grace of his stride was the result of a conscious decision. It was thought that the sight of a man walking should be a minor delight. Eventually this gave way to greater concerns, though it never fell completely from view. Walking ultimately was developed into a form of maintenance. When a body's pace was properly set body functions were at an optimum. The internal organs could work at the highest possible level. The heart moved nutrients around precisely as needed while keeping the arteries and veins clear, and the lungs would take in the exact amount of air the body called for. In fact, all organs eventually performed far better than human intelligence at one time believed possible. Rather than with prescribed exercises, the gait of the man is what kept them so. Constant maintenance of this sort was a must: it was fully expected that this man would live forever.

Over hills, past trees and brush, even nimbly through a brook the journey of the man continued. Terrain changes brought some adjustment to his walk, and he slowed somewhat going uphill while neatly gliding over the brook. Whatever obstacles entered his path were easily overcome as his physical abilities were more than a match for nature's fancies. To be sure, a tree might cause an occasional sidestep. Yet once around a blockage the direct path was resumed.

After uncounted miles and a few hours time a compound appeared in the distance. It was spread over a small area and contained several structures. They were arranged in two rows split by a path which itself led to a large building centered to the far end of the encampment. Short paths led from each smaller structure onto the main walkway. Every place was white and enclosed and squarish; each had its own value. But this was of no consequence. The man had use for only the large one.

Once he arrived at the compound the man stepped onto the main path, which was as white as the buildings. The surrounding grass was vivid green and respectful of the walk's right of way. The man strode to the center of the large structure to a door exactly as wide as the path. It opened obligingly an instant before he reached it. He did not have to break his stride in passing through.

The door opened into a large room quite probably a lobby. The white material which made up the path spread out to cover the floor of the room, and even the walls and ceiling. A faint light now shone through it, more intense in some areas than others, thus making the room splotched with gray. There were benches along the walls and an oval counter in the center of the floor. Counter and bench alike were the same white stuff of most all else. The room had no windows; the door behind the man, now closed, was opaque.

At the far left corner of the room was a ramp leading downward. The man proceeded upon it, and the ramp curved gently until he was in the basement of the structure directly below the entrance. A series of vertical lines marked off sections on the walls, and each section was slotted about two-thirds of the way from the ceiling. The man went randomly to one of the slots. As he reached it the slot spit out a packet of yellow pills, blue sticks, and white capsules. Mission accomplished.

After taking his supplies in hand the man turned smartly and went back up the ramp. Back in the main room he only barely hesitated before heading straight for the nearest bench and laying down. He had killed a lot of time this day due to the extra activity of finding a food station, and needed a bit more sleep than usual. The message had been momentarily vague and thus the hesitation. It wasn't anything a few additional minutes rest wouldn't cure.

The man woke at mid-dawn, precisely as he had every morning before. His body was completely rested. The routine began anew.

When breakfast had ended the man rose, the wrinkles in his outfit smoothing themselves against his body. From a two inch thick white turtleneck collar the suit in one piece covered the entirety of the man except for his hands. There was no evidence of a zipper, snaps, ties, or any other imaginable closing devices. At the feet the suit was slightly thicker, yet this was unnoticeable on sight. The turtleneck was irrevocably attached to the rest of the outfit, and the outfit was as white as the turtleneck. Except for the spot just below the left knee.

After being notified of this blemish the man went out the opaque door as it slid deferentially aside. He passed the first two structures without a glance, then turned sharply onto a side path towards the second building on the right. As commonly understood the man did not 'know' what he was doing, but as that may be he was seeking a change of uniform. There should be one in the building he now entered.

The structure was not as large as the main building but was ample for its purpose. It consisted of one room full of uniforms. They were hanging on racks situated neatly in rows running front to back from the man stood. Stylistically the suits matched the one he wore. The difference was in the turtleneck. Left to right in the room were four rows of black collared suits, then four with violet, then blue, green, red, orange, and yellow. None, however, were white.

During the time in which the uniforms were made humanity had been divided into large groups. The color of the turtleneck indicated the group membership of the wearer. Black identified the lowest, violet the level above, and so forth. Plenty of each grade of outfit was available. But white: there simply weren't any white collared suits to be found.

Impassive, the man's eyes roamed past each row of clothes. Not finding what he wanted he turned crisply and left. There was no point in checking the other buildings. They would not have what he needed and the man by some sense realized that. What he would never realize was the futility of finding another outfit like what he wore. His was the only one ever made.

The man returned to the door of the main building and turned right, leaving the place at a precise right angle to where he had entered. The compound was quickly behind him. He had no instructions on where to go; he would deal with events as they played out. That was how his life went: always concerned with the moment, never anticipating, never sensing, that another moment would come. It was a form of eternity: every instant was forever, negating the importance of the past and blind to a future.

Thus the man continued his journcy, never knowing where he was going but quite certainly going somewhere. At about the middle of the morning he came to a stream moving briskly down a hillside. The water was clean and clear, fairly sparkling in the sunlight.

The man stopped at the edge of the stream, initially for only as long as it would take to determine where to cross. As he stood waiting he noticed the babbling noise the stream made. It was something new to him, and though the impassivity on his face would never have given it away the man was curious. Slowly he lowered himself into a squat so that he might hear better. This was an unconditioned response: but, then, curiosity was an unexpected condition. The sound of the water was pleasing and comforting: the man's muscles relaxed just a little. As the sparkling caught his eye the man began to watch the water flow. The sound and the movement seemed to him connected. It was just a vague idea within him, but was the closest the man had yet come to a thought.

The man lowered his hand into the water. Immediately he withdrew it. The cold was the culprit: the man had never experienced a change in temperature before. Soon, however, the shock died out and he again put his hand in the stream, slowly and much more deliberately. Once adjusted to the cold the man held his hand in place for quite a long while, content to feel the water move around and past it. He turned his hand, and the water flowed between his fingers.

The man cupped his hand and raised it out of the stream. Most of the water it drew fell away: he stared intently at what remained in his hand. With a circular motion he sloshed what had been left back into the stream. He brought up a new handful to his mouth and drank. It was purely an accident.

And what an accident! The feel of the water in his mouth, the experience of it passing down his throat, the oddity of it spreading throughout his stomach. It was nice; refreshing; different. Totally different from the chalky dryness of the mineral imbedded drink he was accustomed to having occasionally. He took another drink, and had started to take a third when order was restored. Dropping the last handful of water, the man raised himself. Moving silently along the shore he came to a low part of the stream and walked through it. The man left the stream perfectly behind, as though it ceased to exist.

Then it was lunchtime. The man sat down passively and ate. The food was dull and uninteresting, but it provided the nutrients the body needed. That was all that mattered.

The man sat for a moment when he was finished. His situation was being analyzed prior to the resumption of his trek. A series of calculations ended with the determination a change of direction was in order. There was a problem in a compound which was a few days away; it was at a forty-five degree angle from where the man had been walking. With no acknowledgement the man was gone, exactly forty-five degrees from where he came.

The terrain began levelling off slowly but surely. This made no conscious difference to the man, but it did allow him to cover more ground. Over one hill, then a second and a third he went, crossing larger areas of flat ground in between. Before long he came upon another stream. The man failed to take any notice of it, marching straight through the water where their paths intersected. His feet did not get wet: the covering extending from his uniform saw to that. Then the man happened into an apple orchard. It was unkempt, with the grass between the trees a couple of feet high and the trees themselves badly in need of pruning. Obviously, it had not been worked for a long time.

Outdoor farming had ended long before and nature was painstakingly reclaiming her land. Farming had died because the need for natural foods had been eradicated. Artificial foods, the blue sticks and yellow pills, could be produced quickly and efficiently. They were otherwise advantageous because they were easy to store, lasted indefinitely, but most importantly because they lacked the impurities of natural foods.

An impurity could be almost anything. Perhaps a given foodstuff held too much water, the salt content was unacceptably high, or the minerals and vitamins weren't mixed just right. Then, also, to get the correct amount of proteins, vitamins, and minerals required the eating of many kinds of natural foods. This wasn't so with the man-made stuff. Men could be provided with everything necessary for the efficient activity of the human body without waste. This saved time, energy, and effort, replacing the element of chance involved in balancing nutrients.

The man started down an aisle of the orchard, and most likely would have gotten through the place without incident if it weren't for the tree which had sprung up in the center of the row. He had seen it well ahead of time, but as was his standard practice made no attempt to alter his course until he was directly upon it. As he began to step around the tree a light breeze caused an apple hanging at eye level to move.

The man stopped to look at the apple. The deep redness of the fruit, accented by a spot of sunlight toward the top front side of it, made for an engaging sight. Though his expression was of stone the man was quite definitely tempted by the object. Perhaps it was being offered to him?

A rustling sound among the leaves signalled the arrival of another breeze and with it just enough power to shake the apple from its branch. The man's eyes followed its quick descent to the ground. He stared for a moment after it came to rest before bending down to pick the apple up. He tried squeezing it—it was firm. Then the man remembered something, and that was his experience with the water. He brought the apple to his mouth and bit it.

Apple juice spurted onto his face. Only the slightest jerk of his head as he drew the apple back gave clue to the man's start. He looked intently at the fruit, not comprehending what had happened. The man noticed the two semi-circles indicative of the teeth he did not know he had. He bit the apple again, taking a chunk of it into his mouth.

For several moments the man simply let the piece of apple sit on his tongue. It was sweet and delicious, especially to a palate which did not realize that something one ate could be enjoyable. When the taste began to fade the man rolled the chunk around his mouth, momentarily restoring its strength. Eventually no amount of rolling had any effect. It was then that the man broke the bit of fruit with his teeth.

He was handsomely rewarded. His reaction was involuntary, the barest of a smile sneaking onto his face. The man began to chew thoroughly, until every ounce of taste was gone.

After swallowing what he had the man quickly took two more bites, intent on devouring the apple as fast as possible. He chewed and swallowed and bit off more, his face growing more openly emotional, looking nearer to human than at any other point in his life. As he ate the man studied his surroundings, seeing things near and distant, and observing the landscape as he had not before, as diverse, colorful, and attractive. The view was always missed when he took his regular meals. He finished his first apple and attacked a second with the intensity of a man who hadn't eaten in days.

Abruptly the man stopped. This wasn't right, he should not be eating this way or these things. So said a voice which was irrevocably part of him, yet somehow other than he. These are bad, it said. Forget them.

But the man did not want that. Although he was not able to clearly formulate a thought, the man was reluctant to obey. He liked the apples and he wanted to eat the one in his hand. In open defiance the man took it to his mouth, as a child would challenge a parent. But he was prevented from eating. Again he tried, to no avail. This was obviously no physical struggle. The battle was purely mental, perhaps best interpreted as a crisis of conscience. The man's face reflected a deep internal confusion.

Within minutes things were set straight. Victory went to that which was other than he. Stoically the man observed the apple, before lowering it to his side. Mechanically releasing his grip, the apple fell to join the residue of the other fruits rotting on the topsoil.

CHAPTER TWO

On a clear morning a few days later, the man was making his way through what had at one time been a pasture. Cattle had grazed on it but cattle were no longer needed. Yet, interestingly, there was no evidence of bovine remains. All animals had been gathered up and taken off to be killed, their flesh and bones destroyed out of sight and hopefully out of mind.

The planet had been rid of animals simply because animals were not necessary to the perfection of man. But what of their beauty, as the song of the bird? Or loyalty, as the dog to his master? Or their universality, that they should exist for the sake or enjoyment of all people? Beauty, loyalty, universality and their kin became interpreted as romantic notions with no grounding in reality. There was no cause for allegiance to abstraction. Well, why not get rid of the plants? They were fortunate. More pressing projects arose.

At the edge of the pasture a forest began. There where the grass was low and the timing right the man stopped for his mid-day meal. As he ate he paid no attention to the things around him.

Soon after lunch the man came into a clearing where the vegetation was sparse and there were patches of dry, barren ground. Many rocks of varying sizes and shapes were scattered about the little plain. Most were smallish, and just laying on the dirt. A few were imbedded in the earth, their jagged edges pointing upward or outward. One large rock was barely in the man's path, but the fact meant nothing to him personally.

Yet as he passed it by a sharp point tore a tiny rip above his left ankle, below the spot closer to his knee. The man's uniform was showing weaknesses unexpected, presumably caused by age. His skin was also opened: a cut which almost matched the tear in his clothing. Blood oozed slowly, leaving tiny red spots on the uniform near the wound. The man did not flinch; in fact, he didn't even notice any trouble. Such little noise and minor pain were unintelligible.

It was during supper that the accident came to his notice. The man sat in a position which exposed the injury. The spots of blood were dried, and the redness was lighter on his suit than his skin. The man reached to touch the red dots, and realized the ones on the uniform were stiffened while those on his skin flaked away. He toyed with his wound, and discovered the blood which came from his body after he would pick a spot clean. All told, there was nothing for him to be concerned with. He was assured the wound would take care of itself.

On the afternoon next the man was trudging across the center of a large flat field. It was covered with short, gnarled grass, similar to what would be found on a putting green. The field had been made for the purpose of mobility tests. The need had long passed yet the grass remained unchanged, a tribute to its develop-ed perseverance. Far to the man's right were rolling man-made hills and a dry, rocky section of the test area. He saw them but took no real notice. They were parallel to his line.

Once he was about two-thirds of the way across the field the man caught something in the lower periphery of his vision. It was moving along with him, and nothing registered as to what it could be. Steady, measured looks at it did not help the determination. Finally the man stopped, and the thing stopped too. When he resumed his pace the thing again took with him. It matched the man's stride exactly, fluid and graceful. The man found this dis-quieting; he was too used to a singular monotony. Since he was getting no help in solving the mystery, the man began to experiment.

The man stopped abruptly a second time, as did his partner. He took one step; the movement was complimented. Next he tried something unusual: a direct sideways step. Without hesitation the object side-stepped. The man was slowly figuring out that its motions were somehow dependent on his. He raised his arms out from his sides: another match. The man wiggled his fingers; he turned his head purposefully right to left to right. All these actions were acknowledged with identical efficiency. The man was now certain the thing relied on him. Or at least, as certain as it was possible for him to be. His knowledge was fuzzy, as when you know you've done something but feel the need to check it again. The man knew, but still questioned, the fact.

He lowered his arms to rest position, making sure his counterpart did the same. Then the man drew his arms together in front of him, his hands touching at the thumbs with the palms facing down. It was an awkward position as his fingers pointed towards the ground, but before the man thought to change his hands around he became fascinated with the lines and folds in his palms. He collapsed his hands into loose fists, watching the lines sharpen until they disappeared. The man observed, to his liking, that his left and right hands were mates. He grasped his left wrist, as did his imitator.

Slowly, surely, and wonderingly, the man looked down his left arm, following it to his shoulder, then his chest, stomach, legs, and feet. Letting go of his wrist he touched his right hand to his chest. He pressed on it, afterwards pressing on his stomach. It was curious that one was not as solid as the other yet still firm. Then the man saw the cut on his ankle. He pressed hard on it and felt a tolerable but definite pain. He made no sound, and the pain was quickly gone.

With a renewed interest the man stared again at what was in front of him. Beginning at his feet (as that was where the thing touched him) the man followed the outline of the form in inverse order to how he had studied his own body. Whatever it was it matched his shape, although it was noticeably oblong. The man bent down to touch it and was puzzled to touch the ground. As he stood back up the man watched severely as the thing stretched out and away from him. The outline was surely something of its own merit, but the lack of solidity suggested otherwise.

The man stood, silent and perplexed. He then noticed the brightness around the edge of the figure. Turning around, the man saw nothing save the sharp greenness of what he had just covered. There was an immense light above the ground, causing him to turn skyward. Squinting harshly, the man realized for the first time the existence of the sun. He turned forward to see if the figure on the ground was still with him. It was. The ball in the sky caused the image on the earth, with him as intermediary.

Since the arousal of curiosity the man had stepped onto the road to rationality. But thinking on the part of an individual was problematic: there was no telling where it could lead. Rather than allowing him to mull over the subject at hand directions began coming down to the effect that he must move on. The man was informed that the thing on the ground was of no importance. Standing and dwelling over it was idle. One was best off moving ahead.

Yet it was nice to be lost in thought, and the man was pleased to have figured the thing out. He resisted the impulse given, but after what amounted to intense badgering he did walk on. The man was satisfied to see his companion resume the journey as well. As they reached the edge of the testing range they met a tree. The image moved up the trunk of it as the man passed. He saw this and reached to touch his friend. A half smile thinly parted the man's lips.

As the man went deeper into the trees he kept his eye on his travel mate so much as the sun and taller vegetation allowed. Whenever his companion left the man almost felt a loss. Yet it always eventually returned, so that its arrivals were anticipated by the man. He became conscious of the changes in form his friend might take, as it stretched out on flat sections of the earth while ruffling across the leaves of the bushes by the way. The man and the form were always connected. The most profound idea this taught the man was of change with recurrence, of continuity over time. His life had been continuous enough and had certainly taken time, but this had been unnoticed. He had been victimized by the dry, anesthetic dullness of the isolated moment.

Still, the man was slipping back into that mode when he cleared the forest and was upon a small lake. It was clean and calm, with hardly any movement on the surface of the water. The lake was directly in his path, forcing the man to veer left. He made his turn as he reached the shoreline, but kept close to the water as he walked. A minute later it struck him that something was wrong. His partner was no longer alongside. Instead, there was a totally different figure.

This development confused the man. The new figure moved with him as the old did, but it was not like the other at all. He seemed connected to it but he wasn't sure, because the line of the ground at the water's edge obscured where any meeting point would be. Whereas the other was simply a darkened figure this one had color, white, yellow, and gold. The man extended his arms and wiggled his fingers: so did the thing on the lake. He took a step: the move was matched. The man then knew they were part of each other. What he could not know was that he was closest he would ever be to meeting another man.

As he went down to one knee the man noticed the other image mock him. Initially he just looked things over, verifying the thing as a reality. The man put a finger to the water and sent soft ripples across the surface, causing the figure to roll. When the little waves died he caused a new set, interested at the effect. Then he studied the image more closely. The man noted the whiteness which was most of the figure. The three spots of gold and the one of yellow were also prominent in his deliberations. Two objects at the center top of the figure, right below the yellow, particularly concerned him. They seemed. . . odd.

Impulsively the man touched his chest with his right hand. The image touched itself identically. Still holding his hand to his body the man looked down, seeing if he was touching white like the figure. The man ran his hand over every part of him which was white, and found he could use the image as a guide. He took the time to look at his hands: soft gold in color, like those on the water. The man turned his palms toward the image, and the image offered its palms to the man. The lines of the image matched those on his own hands.

The man studied the face of the other. He saw the mouth, the nose, the sharply squared jaw. Then the yellow. He pressed his hand to the top of his head as the figure did to the yellow. And next, a shudder went through the man. He had been uneasy for the last few minutes, and the discomfort had risen to complete fruition. All the while he had been studying the image it had been studying him. He did not like the feeling.

Deliberately the man raised himself to a standing position. Then an unexpected but welcome calm fell over him. He puzzled about the thing in front of him, wondering what to make of it. Then the answer came, rushing forth as a great revelation always does. On the water was a reflection, a picture he had never before seen, and one he would never forget.

He had discovered his physical self.

CHAPTER THREE

The man was running hard and fast. The lake was many miles behind him, out of sight if not completely out of mind. He was now a study of pure human speed, effortlessly shooting over level ground and low hill as if there were no difference. To his eyes, if he would have taken time to notice, everything was a blur, the trees and rocks and barren earth rising amidst the grasses shading together thoroughly.

His organism was in the process of testing itself, checking the systems for signs of weakness. A certain amount of stamina was required of the body; the man was in his third mile and ought to be able to do two more without any significant laboring. His legs dug forward furiously, virtually scaling the ground. His arms pumped rhythmically front to back, and his stride was the picture of synchronization.

On occasion the man would have to perform other feats. In due time he would test his strength, his senses, and his manual dexterity. Running was on the schedule today, and run he did. Lung capacity, cardiovascular condition, muscular efficiency, and joint and arterial stress were all under the gun. All were performing well above standard.

After completing his fifth mile the man began a long, measured slowdown. It was as a shadow falling under the movement of the sun, slow and exacting, unnoticed until it was gone. His sixth and seventh miles were decelerations, his eighth a normal walk. Taking his time in the transition prevented a shock to his system. The man was assumed to be perfect, but that unfortunately didn't mean he was indestructible.

He wasn't even sweating as he ended his exercise. He didn't breathe heavily and had no need of composing himself. Walking was again his regimen. The man was back on normal maintenance.

Soon he was told it was time for a liquid supplement, which would be found at the compound to which he was headed. The man passed through a small wood then over a shallow rise when, directly in front of him, appeared a compound identical to the one he had seen before. He stepped onto the main walkway and was quickly inside the building at its end. Down the ramp, at random but decisively choosing a slot, the man took the cup that met his hand and dumped its contents down his throat. He sat the cup on the slight edge below the access slot, and the slot obligingly reclaimed it.

Then it was time to rectify the problem for which he was sent. The man doubled back up the ramp and into the lobby, heading directly to the counter which occupied its center. The counter had been for receiving guests and dispensing information. This was for the benefit of the lesser forms of humanity, the blues and violets who needed verbal or written instruction. They could not know on their own where food could be found, or what other buildings they might need to visit. It wasn't that such people were looked down upon but more the acknowledgement of poor, backward souls who required special aid. The counter had not been manned in ages.

The structure was simple enough, and was covered top to bottom with the same material which was on the floor, walls, ceiling, indeed every other object in the room. There were no set demarcation points as to where the furniture or the counter began. From the floor to an object was a precise quarter-circle; as a matter of fact, there were no corners per se anywhere. Wherever one should be expected or an edge appropriate instead were quarter or half-circles. After the counter had risen a short way was a second quarter-circle which was the underneath to a ledge. At the end of this was a half-circle leading the way to the counter top. A third quarter curve turned the top downward for the inside counter wall. On the inside wall were shelves, each with their own curved pronouncements. The entrance to the counter was to the left of the man.

As he entered the man ran his hand along the counter top. There were no impurities. Cupping his hand, he followed the top's quarter-circle part of the way around. It was actually rather comfortable, and seemed to massage his fingers and palm as they slid across. The man stopped his hand at one point and began to squeeze. The material gave little before holding firm. It was fantastically strong, more so than the muscles in the man's hand, which were no weak things themselves. Eventually he tired of the contest and released his grip.

The man stooped down to peer into the shelves. They were deep enough to hold a standard size brochure exactly. Interestingly the shelves were not dark, their walls radiating a soft light. The man stuck his hand into the shelves one at a time as he came to them, discovering the problem in the fifth he tried. An errant brochure remained. Without any thought he crumpled it up, and tossed it into an opening at the corner of the room.

He started to leave but unexpectedly did not. Something opened in his mind, and the man began instead to venture around the lobby, touching and observing many of the artifacts within. He noted all the common qualities: the general illumination, the sturdy whiteness which covered everything, and the precise curves and perfect flatness wherever they occurred. Yet soon differences came into focus. Shape, mostly, offered a contrast between objects, and there were the patches of gray where the light failed to shine through adequately. The concept of inequality faintly registered inside the man.

The man sat on one of the benches along a wall, unsure what he might do next. The other within him wanted him to leave; this was the one thing the man was sure he didn't want. He was prone to have a tour of the compound, to explore the area and see if the other structures were like this one. Finally he elected to do just that. Calmly yet firmly he was informed the other buildings were not his concern. The point was ignored, if with some odd reservation.

Leaving the main structure resolutely, he entered the second building on the right. As expected—the man could now anticipate somewhat—it was full of uniforms. The uniforms were arranged as those in the earlier compound were. Only one difference existed: instead of simple orange and yellow necked outfits there were six colors, three shades of orange, and three of yellow, each lighter than the one before. The lightest of the yellow was wispy enough it could have almost been mistaken for white. They had become more precise as time went on, concerned with improvements within as well as between ranks.

The man turned and left the tailor's shop, going straight to the building across the aisle. Inside were many instruments, all white and attached irrevocably to the floor. It was a clinic. The instruments were easy enough to use if not comprehend: stand on one for weight, against another for height, grasp a handle for metabolic readings, and so forth. Yet the man could only have discovered their functions by accident, and at any rate would not have been told the meanings of those functions. By standing on the scale he would be informed only that all was well, and nothing more, not so much as what he weighed. It was not important for the man to know his height or weight or heart rate. The man tired of the place, and left.

Once outside, he stood to consider his next move. The man was making choices on his own, albeit on the level of a tempered Freudian Id. His thoughts were childish, barely above mere impulse. But he knew he could freely go to any of the structures around him as he wished. There wasn't much to help his choosing, with all the buildings the same save the main one. In the end proximity sent him to the very next white mass. Why? Well, why not?

It was an exercise center, and the floor turned itself into a variety of equipment. A stationary run, with no handles or sidebars, occupied the center of the room. It would start under the pressure of a foot. A variation

on the rowing machine sat closer to the entrance, and there were polygo-
nal weights in a corner. In all, there was something or other designed to
tone any given muscle in the body. The man was unconcerned with any at
the moment. He exited without further observation.

The clinic and exercise center were probably the most important
facilities in the compound. The food center was a requirement but had
no direct bearing on the progression of the experiment. If the human
form was to be perfected there had to be ways of measuring and
increasing its perfection. Genetics were critical as well, but such questions were handled elsewhere. The compounds dealt with the creatures
who already existed, and whatever data they collected did go to the
genetic files for reference purposes. But perfecting an individual man
wasn't nearly so important as perfecting Man.

A perfection was viewed as any measurable and sustained increase in
test grades within specific systems. Thus any improvement in metabolic
efficiency, overall bodily appearance, synchronization of movements,
etcetera, all broken into parts, constituted the continued improvement
of the species. Setbacks were rare, and almost always within the lower
levels. Disease may have stalked a green or someone below. By the time
of the red collars the immune system was able to ward off even the common cold.

The next building contained a pharmacy. On the left hand wall were
a series of slots which accessed drugs exactly as food could be. Across
the back of the typical single room was a straight counter opened at one
end. Again this was for the less perfect, a place where they could have
physical contact with a druggist. Along the right wall were benches.
With the luxury of personal contact came the anger of the wait.

Odd shaped glass objects took up the wall behind the counter. The
light was noticeably brighter behind them than the other walls. The
glasses were empty, their contents used up or moved behind the left wall
long ago. The man approached the counter for a closer look at them. To
say they were beautiful would understate their beauty. Smoothly curved

and precisely though variously shaped, these crystal clear bottles were of the purest, most refined glass as could be had.

There were no markings on the glass whatsoever: the worker always knew what each held. The man went behind the counter and reached for one, a small sphere atop a larger with a vague waistline between. But instead of clutching it he knocked it to the floor. The glass did not break. It actually bounced, a tiny, excuse me bounce, and faintly echoed. Strength was one of its primary qualities. After a second, tinier bounce, the object was silent.

The man carefully picked it up. Its smoothness did not escape his fingertips; its proportionality registered in him also, top sphere to bottom a 1:2 ratio. He stuck his hand inside so far as it would allow, and became aware of transparency. The man tipped the glass over and over slowly, studying it from several angles. He ran a finger around the opening, curious as to why it was there and never considering it as an access point. Taking the opening to his eye he looked through the bottom of the jar, dryly amused at the distortions it created of the room. The minute he was satisfied with his findings the man returned the object to its place.

A tall cylindrical glass was set slightly apart from the others, enough so the man couldn't help but notice it. He picked it up gently, that he would not upset it. The man saw immediately the similarities with the other glass. How it differed was a matter of aesthetics, and he somehow grasped the point. The double sphere was marvelous but also complex. The tube had all the quality of that other object plus the advantage of simplicity. The rest of the objects had to be examined carefully, their forms, while fascinating on their terms, still somewhat fighting themselves. The tube was seen up then down, in one motion, as one unit.

The man toyed with the cylinder for a moment or two. It was comfortable to just hold it in his hand, being quite easy to grip. He put the object to his lips, and as luck would have it exhaled across the mouth. The man drew back quizzically; there was a small sound, a shy lyric, and he knew not why. But it was pure, clear, and lightly resonant. It went on in his head long after it had died in reality.

Stupefied, the man returned the glass to his lips, and with his breath the sound emerged. Although his face was as rock-like as ever, he was inwardly pleased. He then blew wholeheartedly across the tube, sending out such a forceful note as to awaken every glass in the place. The ensuing tone was intense and wondrously shrill. The man reactively closed his eyes and was lost in the sound. He listened sedately as the room quieted. He produced the chord once more, to live with him forever.

When the second tone had physically gone the man placed the cylinder back among its siblings. It never occurred to him that he could have kept it, and there was that part of him which was content with the lack of foresight. As he stepped from behind the counter the man took a last survey of the pharmacy. Here was his symphony, his first indelible mark on the world. Turning to leave, he was appreciatively let out the door.

Once outside the pharmacy the man stopped. He let his eyes follow the compound around, and saw how each side of the center aisle matched the opposite. The compound was ordered, symmetrical. This was supposedly comforting surroundings, and the man would not have noticed it differently before this day. But it seemed to him forced and institutional. At least, that would describe his feelings approximately enough. He was beginning not to like it.

The next structure was a laundry, of no use to anyone now, and the man left it without consideration. The sixth building was a bunkhouse: he took no measure of it. The seventh was empty save for a podium centered a few feet in front of the back wall. The building had been used for assemblies, and the echoes of the last speech had since faded. The place next door was hollow, its interior dismantled and purpose forgotten. The ninth was as victimized as the eighth, with no trace of use. Number ten had been a welcome center, a small scale of the main building but without a basement.

The man was tired. It was not expressly because of the run, though that certainly was a contributing factor. Positively it was not due to the explore: the energy spent on that was virtually nil. The problem was more something the man could not have grasped at the time. The entity which was inside him comprehended it all too well and was not about to clue him in. He was afflicted with mental strain. Deep within the man, far deeper than the entity cared to probe, something of individuality had lay dormant. Awakening slowly and steadily the mind of humanity, the mind of this human, was starting to live for itself. Like anything else which goes long unused it had burned out quickly, revitalization to come only through rest. Sleep tonight was for his mind much more than his body.

CHAPTER FOUR

The entity within the man worked feverishly throughout the night. The situation was serious, but far from beyond control. All that was needed was to employ a highly advanced sleep learning technique. The entity began to poison the mind of its host. "The glass objects just sit, not able to do anything. They have no real function. What is the sound, then? It reverberates into nothingness. You are a being, a perfect being who will survive, will continue to be, able to do useful work. Running proved your perfection: the body did very well, better than it had to, better than it should have. When other tests are done it will be even more obvious. You are not a man, but Man, superior to all else." The entity had had to deal with a man who had stumbled into the initial stages of rationality. His mind was open to experience. First, then, his mind must be closed, and Pride would accomplish this.

In his sleep the man could not compete. The power of suggestion easily overran his weak resistance. By morning the entity was dominant, for along the way it had managed to convince the man to accept its pre-eminence. Had he not been cared for thus far? The man overslept but the entity, cautious, ignore the gaffe.

The man sat up, and was not in the least concerned with where he was or how he'd gotten there. The compound meant nothing to him, and he had no recollection of the previous day. Breakfast lost any importance; it was no more than what he did at that point. He was the epitome of noncomprehension.

Soon enough the man left the camp, swiftly and certainly. In no time he was back on track. He needn't consider his next move. Directions would come whenever there was a task at hand. His thinking would be done for him. Indeed, that was the chief job of the entity inside him.

There was no reason for men to have to think. It had been realized years before that human thought was often vague and garbled, and therefore without a point. Imprecision resulted, and imprecision could not be tolerated. In the drive to refine the species it was too much to risk an individual weakness which could lead to the failure of the attempt. Initially it was believed the answer was to educate all people thoroughly, so that each could rise to his natural level of competence and placed accordingly. That proved to be time consuming and costly, taking twenty years and more (dependent on the case) while costing tens of thousands of dollars. Money eventually was eliminated as a factor: it went out of existence as cumbersome and unnecessary. But the time— so long, and still with no guarantee of success.

As a result the power of thought was taken from the human and given to the mechanical. Computerized thought became the way of the world, its quickness and efficiency ever increasing, until it had expanded to the level of a substitute for the human mind. The idea was sold and bought as a way out of the drudgery of having to sit and figure things out, and to avoid the hassle of committing bits of information to memory. When the touch of a button could bring forth nearly any fact or figure, from the time the sun would set to the resolution of a difficult calculus equation, there seemed little need of individual mental prowess. Consequently, the reliance on an artificial brain created a weakness in the capacity to question let alone resist changes in direction.

Yet push button access was not all reward: it still suffered the risk of human error. The wrong button might be hit, or the wrong sequence played in request of certain information. Further, what was on file in a databank had to be put there by someone, who could make a mistake in the process, perhaps misreading the script he worked with. It became apparent that rote human involvement had to be done away with entirely.

The death of the mind was already well advanced. But it had to be hurried on even more quickly to avoid significant mistakes. At first a stop-gap solution was employed: a select few were chosen for intensive training in information processing and data recording. The knowledge and skills they required were force fed in the strictest sense, virtually pounded into them through lectures, classwork, and practice sessions on false equipment. Their minds were numbed so that nothing outside of the planned regimen could impress itself upon them. They were to be as ants, working closely in a prescribed and tight order. They were expected to become almost part of their machines. And the system would work well for many years, buying the time necessary for the arrival of the permanent answer.

Chemicals were freely used to control people: so too were genetics. Nerve impulses and therefore brain functions could be stymied or altered with the ingestion of the right substance in the proper dosage. Bloodlines and breeding would help the chemicals along. Eventually right responses became inbred, effectively a regular part of bodily functions. Cellular restructuring held the chemicals in place. Tremendous amounts of training went into developing and implementing the knowledge to carry this out: scientists and doctors were made into automatons just as the information access specialists, whom they typically relied upon.

Never was a doctor a data recorder or retriever. Their duties were kept strictly apart so that the physician would not learn to randomly comb for information or accidently hit on something outside his well defined specialty. Likewise every data recorder was kept in specifically developed information systems from which breakout was unlikely. Mistakes in the purely medical field could be overcome even with the setback of a generation or two. But the rise of a closet philosopher might shred the entire fabric.

The time came when automatic mechanized thought was perfected. There was no longer a question of determining the right answers. It was a matter of having the answers given without even the asking. The new superminds would identify difficulties, analyze and resolve them, instruct the laborers (where robotic means were not available) on what to do, and file the information for later use. A system of these machines was set up in every area of the globe, tied into a central mammoth operation, a primary computer whose location was secret, the few men left both aware of and consenting to the new order wishing to avoid any chance of sabotage. Soon they were gone, their select knowledge less than a footnote in an unwritten history.

The system still would not be complete until it was part of the physical makeup of each person. The preliminary work made this a snap. People had relied on explicit instruction for so long that they simply reported to a medical facility on demand for special treatments. All remaining generations were effected through the final reworking of human genes. The population was victimized by a medically induced schizophrenia, with their born personalities the subsidiary entities, the junior partners in a global firm.

And so there was this man, this last man, the very junior partner whose boss was always with him, not merely looking over his shoulder but controlling it. The mechanics of the planet were still run from some hidden place, such as they functioned over time, distributing from afar the decades old food which was yet fresh, telling the man where to go and what to, challenging the foliage to encroach on its compounds. It would do so indefinitely.

With a programmed resolution on his face the man walked onward. He fairly trampled the ground with his determined stride. An errant branch from a bush too near the man's path was scornfully (it would seem) kicked away, as though he meant to teach it a lesson.

An occasional pebble or small stone would be mashed into the earth if it was unfortunate enough to come underfoot. The entity had its masterpiece well under control.

The man continued his unknown journey, never thinking of before or after. The moment was always there for him, and he took it, as it was all that was offered. He stopped to eat his lunch on the sunny side of a hill, and his ability to withstand the sun's ultraviolet rays was promptly tested. Was there any doubt he would pass? When the test was complete and his three course meal over, the man rose majestically, the sun a sharp white on his forehead. He resumed his course precisely on line with the morning trek. He would walk it forever unless an ocean or the unforeseen prevented it.

For quite a while, perhaps a week, the man went forward, stopping only as prescribed. If it knew of anything beyond the task at hand the entity likely would be happy at its triumph. Yet like the creature in whose body it rode the entity was unacquainted with emotion and time, really more so than the man himself. So perfect was its development that there was no chance whatsoever of it being overcome. The man, however, was different. The germ of human frailty was still some small part of him. It was the distinction between creation and refinement. The power within the man would never change: a quirk of fate might somehow alter his self.

Fate, as might be expected, was playing her hand like an expert. The man's route was soon matched by a man-made waterway about ten feet wide. It had curved in graciously from his left, as though it were a carpet laid out for him. The water was shallow and crystal clear, its bed the same material found on every other man-hade object the man had so far found, the whiteness more brilliant underwater. The artificial bed rose from the stream to form sidewalks on each side. One of them coincided with the man's path.

The stream was an irrigation ditch, and the man followed it for about a half a mile. There were no breaks save one, a tributary which shot off to the man's right, forming a 90 degree angle with the mother stream. The tributary was slightly narrower, making it appear to run faster than the original, which was more casual in its flow. The offshoot ran straight as a needle to parts unknown, disappearing into the far horizon. This made no impact on the man, who purposefully crossed a sidewalk bridge constructed at the intersection of the two lines. The bridge was flat rather than crowned, and as wide as the walk. It was as if the sidewalk ignored the interruption of the tributary. The bridge would never flood over; the water level could never rise, controlled as so many other things were. The waterways were never asked for more than they could deliver.

The man continued forth with a square-shouldered, even stride. Despite being harnessed the water retained its innate qualities. The water winked and sparkled and rolled, little wavelets engaged in the waltz as the stream moved on, the sun gamely highlighting the motions. The clear liquid never begged to be seen. It was merely asserting its presence, asking for the consideration it deserved. But such was not forthcoming. Following quiet orders, the man would not recognize the stream.

Finally he and the water parted company. The ditch veered away to the left as smoothly as it had came. Keeping to his line the man exited the sidewalk at the exact point he ought. The grass was growing a bit higher now, and wildflowers began to appear, here and there at random. A few trees encroached on the man's path, forcing swift step-arounds that failed to break his rhythm. The trees were tall and strong, pure green and brown. The flowers were petite and lovely in a variety of colors. Even the college green of the grass was eye catching. Unnoticing, the man strode past all of it.

The land cleared into an orchard. It was made up of cherry trees, and was more organized and seemingly better kept up than the apple orchard had been—a trick caused by well bred agriculture. And it was in fact newer. The grass was low and the trees appeared neatly trimmed.

Unknown to the man this was the ultimate destination of the irrigation canal, as tiny white bedded rivulets coursed between each row of trees. If he would but turn his head the man would see cherry trees almost forever.

The man stepped over the small tributaries easily as he moved through the orchard. Although they looked like the larger streams their bases were different, the water able to seep into the earth through more porous walls. The water dropped steadily until the bed ran dry at the end of every run. All the orchard was thus well fed. This place was far from going wild; the entity need not be concerned with another accidental meeting. It simply had to keep its prey heading forward, his eyes locked straight into the distance. The entity and the man were up for a critical exam. But the advantage was to the soulless other. It could openly and directly argue.

The redness of the cherries was sharper than that of the apples. The smallness oddly enough magnified the appearance of the fruits, causing each individual cherry to seem more defined and precise. The surrounding leaves formed a nicely contrasting background, the dark green and bright red nicely accenting one another. Yet the man had been subdued; nature's demands for all intents and purposes did not exist. Occasionally a light breeze caused the smaller branches to sway as it ruffled the leaves. These minor movements brought no meaning to the man's mind. There was no world outside his body.

The man stoically continued across the orchard, deftly stepping over the ninety-first, ninety-second, and ninety-third riverlet. The entire orchard still called for his attention. Every tree within sight proclaimed itself to the world. That they were ignored was of no consequence: they were nevertheless present. Several times the man stepped upon old fruits which had given themselves to the ground. He never knew it.

Eventually he emerged from the trees, having traversed the width of the orchard. He was on a slight upgrade to which his pace was imperceptibly adjusted. The woods about him thickened and thinned in no coherent pattern. Light brush and a few saplings were in his line: the route was easily made passable against their challenges. The man was trailblazing, his arms and legs accomplishing what earlier men would have needed sharp tools for. Twigs snapped, branches bent, leaves ripped from plants from the sheer force of his gait. There could be no doubt where the man had gone. His wake would remain for days.

The forest became increasingly dense. The trees, brown and leafless near the ground, towered above the man. Together with the odd cloud they effectively blocked the sun. A few rays managed to get through just the same, in straight, narrow, parallel lines and at a slight angle to the earth's surface. Nothing was reflected in them, not the slightest dust speck. Just pure, clear sunrays, a testimony to the remarkably clean air. Somewhere on the globe was a purifying plant which kept the air clean while maintaining the right mixture of elements in the atmosphere. A series of stealthily hidden ducts sent nitrogen or oxygen or inert gases wherever they were low, and a like series of gauges were in place to let the central air supplier know when such was the case.

A contest was brewing between the man and an old friend of his. As he walked on a form went in and out of existence. It ran about just in front of him, dancing on the crags in the ground, the figure obscured due to the effect of the trees on the dark brown of the forest floor. The sunlight, whenever it could, sparkled at the edges of the form. The figure was elongated from somewhere near the man's feet. It was difficult for him to tell for certain exactly where it started.

The form steadily reached further ahead, confusing its presence all the more. The sun continued its valiant effort to enhance the vision: there was not an open venue where a ray of light did not bolt through. But the angle was becoming too sharp, the parts of the form too stretched out for perception to be likely in a deep wood. The day was dying and soon nature's ploys would lose their chance with the man. His speed was purposely, deviously slowed. It may have been too late a move, the reduction not quite enough. But any slower a rate would adversely affect the body's efficiency, and the health of the organism came above all else. Ideally the change in stride would keep the man in the forest until bedtime. By morning the sun would lead rather than follow.

The ideal was not in store. The forest ended along a field of short grass and the man plowed straight onto it. Initially the trees behind him were able to block out the remaining daylight, their shadows reaching far into the clearing. But finally the figure had to expose itself. It emerged from the forest slowly, a thin object black upon the ground. Four reedy appendages were tied into a somewhat thicker torso. The man saw the form bend alternately between two parts and sway rhythmically at two others. This seemed to help the totality in its movement.

A question was coming together in the man's mind. There was this thing, and it moved along with him. What is it? The directives came hard and fast to keep going. Persuasive argument would be used if need be, yet that was always the second option. First efforts were to kill curiosity.

The man took several steps more before a slight hesitation caused a hitch in his gait. A vague familiarity was creeping up alongside the steadily pressing question. There seemed a connection between him and the form, yet the man couldn't put a finger on it. The entity had put in place a highly effective mental block to prevent the man's experiences from registering. A grimace took hold of his face as he tried to sort things out.

The man never stopped, though his usual graceful walking was interrupted. This last test was severe, the faint echoes of self taking on a decidedly powerful adversary. Curiosity welled up and prodded, asking for satisfaction. The entity pushed, directed, and prodded in return. Memory was blunted further with chemicals, precise dosages of the necessary serum injected into the man's bloodstream from unknowable sources. The grimacing on the man's face was softening.

And then time came to the aid of the other. The sun dropped low enough that the trees blocked it completely. The figure melted into the surroundings and was gone without a trace. The man resumed his normal pace, steady and sure. The tests were passed albeit not as well as they should have been. No matter; the situation was as it ought to be.

Not very far across the field the forest began again. The man was just into it when he was directed to rest. He laid himself on the ground, facing west. The twilight which he did not comprehend reflected in his eyes before he closed them to sleep.

CHAPTER FIVE

The man felt himself tapped on the upward side of his nose. Whatever had tapped stayed put, causing him an itch. The man reached, still asleep, and brushed it away. A moment later he was hit on his chin, which he unconsciously rubbed. When he was struck a third time perfectly on the lips the man raised his head and shook it, taking something into his mouth with a dart of the tongue. Water. It had begun raining a few hours before daybreak and drops of water were rolling off the leaves of the tree above where he slept, striking him at their pleasure.

For the first time the man realized a change in the weather. It had been under control for many years. Unpredictability and inefficiency had plagued the weather from the beginning of history. Deserts were left where there was not enough moisture, and floods were common where there was too much. At either extreme the land was ruined, and useless land was of no benefit to anyone. There wasn't any reason for nonproductive ground.

Irrigation had dealt a major blow to the deserts. Together with the development of engineered rainfall the barren regions of the earth were made green with vegetation. Taking rain from areas of overabundance allowed those areas to produce a larger variety of foodstuffs. This revolution in agriculture allowed man to feed himself more efficiently than at any point in his existence. The quality of food had been steadily rising in the years immediately before the weather was harnessed, and rose faster afterward. It happened that virtually all people and things could get enough to eat, with the approximate levels of each of the nutrients they required.

The changes had not solved all the problems of agriculture. It had been thought generally better to have an even handed global growth of agricultural products. But the levelling of the world climate hurt the growth of food plants which needed hotter or colder temperatures, or different amounts of moisture, for satisfactory production. For a time these troubles were solved with the use of flooded, cool, humid, or hot indoor farms. Yet all this was before the cause caught up with the process. Such measures became seen as a waste of time and effort. Food could be made which was better than food grown. Both outdoor and indoor farming came to an end. But the new weather survived the storms of human action.

The man brought himself to a sitting position and looked across the field he had traversed the evening before. He was watching the silvery lines which were falling gently to the ground, packed tightly almost as if a mist. Rain would fall at this same rate all day long, allowing the water to slowly work its way into the earth. Occasionally a raindrop would fall on the man's head or hands. He wondered what was happening, his mind shocked to attention by the rain's gentle kisses in the dawn.

The entity within had known the rain would come but could do nothing to stop it. It could, however, affect the organism on which it was a parasite. The man had been sent under cover to reduce the chance of the rain agitating him. That move was in danger of failing, but such was the best that could be done considering the geographic location of the host. The entity would stand guard for now, vigilant towards an opportunity to shut the man down.

The man continued to sit passively, his eyes trained on the rainfall. As yet he had no inclination to move and the entity had no intention of allowing it anyway. So long as there was rain he would sit, his plot of earth relatively dry and comfortable. At least, such was the plan.

No evidence of wind existed. There was rarely any in the rain as an air current too near the ground might adversely affect the distribution of the water. Leaves hung limp on their branches, disturbed only by the irregular direct hits. The shower was driven from venue to venue by winds high in the atmosphere or adjacent fair weather cells. This particular one had been through the area once before, many years ago, falling to the ground with the same deliberateness then as now. There were myriad other showers just like it. Groups of rain roamed the world in set patterns, becoming heavier or lighter as the case might be, replenishing the land and themselves along the route.

Nowhere on earth was there any type of foul weather. Tornadoes did not threaten; indeed, no damaging winds were possible. Golf ball hail had gone the way of the sport. Except at the northern and southern extremities there was no snow, and even at those points blizzards failed to rage. The high seas were freed of the threat of hurricane or gale. The planet was entirely safe for those who would have it.

For the entire morning the man sat watching the rain. It held his attention well; this was a blessing and a curse for that certain part of him. So long as the man remained mesmerized the order to stay put was in no peril. Yet that was a signal of two potential dangers: it implied assent on the part of the man, and gave rise to the chance he would revoke the decision. The entity's position was precarious, but it could do little but ride out the wave and rely on its wits (if that's an appropriate term).

At the proper time the man ate a tasteless lunch: no danger of chance rearing its ugly head as he took his nourishment. All pleasure had been removed from eating; people could not miss what they did not know, and would therefore not demand it. The blue and yellow colors did nothing for the joy of a meal, yet even they had been on their way out towards a dull gray foodstuff, for safety's sake. The only purpose for coloring foods was for the untrained to tell them apart anyway. Eventually it was deemed too trivial a concern, substance overriding appearance.

The man's expression was, as usual, impassive, belying the fact that he was near to a decision. He was going to venture out into the shower. The thing inside him said no, calmly and firmly asserting it was best to stay put. This had no effect on a mind which now needed a reason to obey. The man wanted to know what would happen if he walked into the silver lines. He was told it was unimportant. No, it was important, a question in search of an answer. The man rose beneath the tree and, ducking a branch, was out into the field.

The entity elected to let him go. The man was in such a state that any overt attempts at coercion were pointless, and potentially harmful. It would allow him to feel the rain as it monitored his reactions. Perhaps the study would hold a clue to holding the man in check. If not, there would be other opportunities for a counterattack. He would have to sleep sometime.

At first the man felt only light dottings on his hand, which he held outward slightly to see if he might catch whatever it was that fell. He was nearing the middle of the field and the mistiness around him was almost a fog. The mist appeared to keep a healthy distance, always eight or ten feet in front of him. Pausing, the man looked full circle and saw the mist holding off similarly all around him. He resumed his pace, turning his head slowly left to right and back to center. An odd feeling was rising inside the man. His vision was obscured by the mistiness; the pocket of fog offered a taste of claustrophobia.

Eventually he reached the other side of the clearing. Unsatisfied and disappointed, the man turned to recross it. Walking back, his curiosity about the shower was becoming tainted. The discomfort caused by the ring around him was the villain. The man was able to experience pleasure. This meant he could also experience other emotions.

The man headed steadily back towards the shelter of the overnight side. The feeling of being hemmed in grew more acute. He found he was in a bubble which was shrinking noticeably as he moved forward. His uneasiness increased. The sides of the ring were inching upon him;

there even seemed to be something closing down on the top of his head. It was pressing down ever more emphatically, until the sensation turned into a physical feeling. The man's ears were plugging. The walls continued inward, tightening onto his body, virtually clenching it. He was pulled forward and pushed roughly by something he could not see. His vision blurred, and lapsed into whiteness. He began to suffocate: he felt as if something was being forced down his throat. The man involuntarily quickened his pace. The grip was powerful, and he felt no chance of breaking it. Pain. He was on the threshold of pain.

The branch he had deftly avoided earlier smacked the man across the face. He jerked his back, then snapped to attention. Ahead of him were the green and brown monuments of the forest. A smattering of water was still on his cheek. The spell was broken. The entity had overplayed its hand. It allowed fear to blossom into panic, where neither it nor the man had any control. It was one of the few miscalculations the entity had ever made.

For several moments the man stood confused. His pulse was far enough above normal that even he noticed his own heartbeat. He considered what was in front of him, making certain it was just a tree. Satisfied to this, he turned back to the clearing. He decided for the time being to avoid further contact with the rain. Ducking under the lower branches of the tree, the man was on his way through the forest.

The floor of the woods was damp but not wet. This dampness was held in by the shield of trees rising high above the earth. The trees did not depend on the damp for survival; their roots laced underground and into the nearest fields for their water. They had little choice, as the giant plants stubbornly refused to allow any significant rain beyond their often broad leaves. An isolated drop or two might discover an avenue between the trees, but most rain was caught and dried out far overhead.

The cold of the damp touched the man's face, and reached into his lungs. He took a deep breath, and his chest seemed to expand greatly as it accepted the forest air. The man liked the scent of the woods; he could not help but pick up on it, he was breathing it in so. The sense of smell was now added to those of taste and sight, and the man enjoyed the sensation. It made for a fine jaunt among the trees.

Claustrophobia was not able to take hold of the man. The trees towered well above and were comfortably spaced. They were not a threat but rather a sanctuary, protecting him with an easy paternal grip. And of course the man's vision was clear. He saw all which was around him with no vertical motion interfering. In the unique stillness he became calm.

When the man was completely through this forest he saw that it continued to rain. Initially the closing in sensation crept up, but he was able to fight it back down. The respite in the woods settled him to where he could affect control over his emotion.

The man came to a ridge and walked along it. He allowed the water to fall on his body, really giving it little thought as he looked ahead and to his left. There was a vast open landscape with the fog-like rain hugging the ground throughout. The green of the distant grass melted into the gray of the clouds at the horizon.

The gray of the clouds. As he looked closely the man realized that the sky was different from how he remembered it. He stood wondering, and he blinked, a slow, measured blink reflective of the vague thought passing through his mind. Why was they sky changed? Why the grayness instead of the bright white ball on the blue background?

Uniformity. The fundamentals of the concept were falling into the man's intellect. The grayness was uniform, exact in shade at all parts of the late afternoon sky. There were no splotches of deep gray as sometimes found in natural showers, no forboding midnight blues as in traditional thunderstorms. There was only an overall sameness, smooth gray sending forth even rainfall.

The man's gaze followed the wide band where the ground and the sky met. He took note of the puffiness along it, a rather odd marring of the world. Then a brightness caught a corner of his eye, and the man turned his head left to inspect it. A yellow triangle was slowly growing from the western end of the horizon. The raindrops began to twinkle and fade.

The man turned his head upwards to look upon the sky. The raindrops which had not yet gone spritzed about his face, until the specks of water formed into crystalline streams running down his cheeks and neck. The clouds purposefully receded, and a few rays of sunlight bolted for the man, gently illuminating his facial features. The man watched intently the passing gray, his golden skin, his wet but vibrant yellow hair, the light touch of the last rain on his face, all bathed in a warm glow. And for just a moment there was an unusual deepness in his eyes.

CHAPTER SIX

The night was restless. The man and the entity were locked in debate. It was both simple and complex, calm and impassioned. The one employed false logic, yet appeared to be reasonable in its entreaties. The other was nearly childish in style, not quite demanding the satisfaction of questions it believed relevant. The situation was not at all conducive to a fitful rest.

Dawn had come and gone long before the man rose. His first impulse of the day considered where he was to go; the entity realized the danger of true choice but was holding back, waiting for helpful data on which to rebut its host's intentions. Now that the sun was again with him the man could see a mountain range in the distance to his left. He was tempted towards it, shadowy and foreboding as it seemed, impassible and yet impressive. The mountains very nearly cast a spell upon him. They were as a painting, appearing flat against the far sky, bold and forcefully colored. But he would not go to them. The order was to proceed, and it did make sense. There was food and shelter in abundance on his current course.

It wasn't that the man obeyed the order so much as he acquiesced in it. He treated the command as though the strict continuation of the journey had been respectfully requested of him and he, holding a concurrent opinion, went along with it. To that which was not him this was disturbing, more so than the events of a day or two before. In waiting out yesterday's rain the man was, at best, only marginally judging the situation. Today he was definitely guilty of a judgment. It was indeed prudent to follow a track safe with all bodily comforts than to forage into the unknown. Of course, the mountains were unknown only because the entity would not release any information about them. The man would never be able to force the issue either.

The man was acting as he was because, the entity postulated, the genetic checks on the system were beginning to fail. It wasn't possible theoretically: yet theories weren't at work in this instance. Nature was laying a siege, and she was of strong will. Countless tricks were up her sleeve, and she might roll them up at any time. The entity wasn't without resources of its own, of course, but was increasingly put on the defensive. The adversaries were well acquainted, and readily able to set one another to the task. All the while their prize was oblivious to the parry and thrust at work within him.

First advantage of the day was to the entity. At about mid-day the man came upon a camp of three buildings. There were no paths to their front doors or between them. He wished to inspect the structures, and encountered no argument. Instead there was the suggestion that the middle one might be the best place to start, the importance of which lay in its centrality. And why not go there first? The others weren't likely to walk away.

The inside of the building was devoid of furniture. Instead there was a right to left maze of six rows which emptied diagonally from where the man entered. He entered the maze after a brief pause, making his way side to side until the exit. There he waited, having been caught by a force he could not know was there. It took a gentle hold on him, relaxing his body as it kept him still, the growing limberness making the diagnosis easier. The man's body was being read so that it might be readjusted, in order to cause his mind to wither. Whatever had been the source of the troubles of late had to be found, isolated, and obliterated.

When the man was released a side door slid open for his departure. There being nothing obviously special in the place with the maze the man left it, to be directed towards an entrance to the adjacent structure. He strode quickly across the grass and was accepted by the sliding door.

In the center of the typical single room was an oval table. The man walked up to it, looked it over, and continued around the oval. He was feeling tired; a short nap could renew him, and the table would suit such a purpose beautifully. He climbed onto it and laid lengthwise, the longest part of the oval exactly right for his height, the narrowness of his torso perfect against the center of the table.

As the man slept another form of examination was taking place. He was undergoing a sort of total X-ray: every cell in his body was checked, the data analyzed then recorded. There was no genetic defect found. This was expected: the original readings had indicated as much, but the findings had to be verified on more accurate equipment to avoid the odd pratfall.

So if the failure was not in the genes it must be due to something able to override them. In a manner this was just as well. No genetic restructuring devices were convenient.

That the genetic makeup of the man was so relatively easily overcome was unexpected but it did not pose an insurmountable problem. In fact the situation could be made right before the man even left the area. Nevertheless, it should not have happened. It lent doubt to the whole project, and the effort could not be duplicated. The products along the way had arrogantly been allowed to fail once their use was past. The total failure or complete success of the endeavor rested squarely on the shoulder of what was on the shoulder of the man.

When the man awoke he felt a keen tingling sensation which permeated his physical being, an aftereffect of the procedure he had undergone. Unsure of himself, the man kept still, waiting to see what may happen next. Gradually the tingling died out, as he tentatively moved his fingers and lifted the arm in which the itchiness was last felt. Satisfied of a return to normalcy, the man sat up and slid off the table.

Standing to one side the man noticed a difference in the light above the table. Shaped oval to precisely match the object below it was a luminescent spot only the barest bit separate from the rest of the ceiling. The doctor was in, eternally ready for the next patient.

The man was sore, generally so over his entire body. Even his insides seemed to hurt. It was not excruciating nor particularly aggravating, yet the soreness was there, touching each part of him quite like the tingling had. This was also due to the examination: how else could one feel once the smallest fraction of the body had been opened, probed, and welded closed. As he took a step the man felt resistance. His joints were stiff and movement was discomforting. A few bends of the knees and twists of the elbows would work it out. By the time the sun touched the man's face the discomfort would be history.

The diagnosis was complete and the prescription had been written. It was time for a visit to the pharmacy. The man went to the final building and stepped inside. He found shelves backed by a high intensity light, stocked with a variety of odd glass forms, all of which were protected by a waist high counter. The man looked around and recalled a similar place. He walked behind the counter and chose a tall glass. He blew across the opening: nothing happened. The man was dismayed at the lack of incident. The entity had beaten him to the draw, seeing that the room had been made inhospitable to sound before the man had entered it.

He did not know what to believe. Memory let sound a note which reality denied. Perhaps the voice inside him was right, and the sounds of the glass had faded permanently, lost in the void of what was not. This was a crushing thought, striking directly at his young and underdeveloped heart. The man felt a genuine loss.

He could not believe it; he would not accept it. Something was wrong, and it was not the glass objects. The man was on the verge of discovering that a trick was being played on him. At least, he was near to making that allegation. Partly he was simply lashing out, indulging himself with the dangerous food which was self pity. Yet it was true the man could sense a deception. It was impossible to hold court, to be able to place blame on that that ought to carry it. The man could not even state his belief with the symbolism called language: he could understand the writing of his era but could neither speak or scribble. But the perpetrator was there, the immorality committed, the deceit known. And possibly a fire was lit in the man.

It was time for his medicine. Stunned and angered, the man had not realized he was approaching the liquid dispensing slot which the entity had his body heading toward. Having arrived a cup was produced, the contents a solution of milky whiteness. The man started to take it, hesitated, the returned his arm to his side. He did not want it and would not drink it. For the moment the man was to be an obstinate child.

The entity was prepared for just such an event. While the man stood ignoring his drink the parasite released into his bloodstream a chemical to combat his stubbornness. The chemical had always been present yet hidden from the man: a rather pointless feature given that he had no way of making such a discovery. Soon enough his medicinal requirements would be fulfilled.

The stuff quickly began to take hold of the man's nervous system. Although he fought with every bit of strength he could muster his right hand came forward and took the cup. His arm moved slowly, trembling softly with perhaps just a quiver. It started to raise the cup to the man's mouth. The fight against the move grew intensely, and the tremors in his arm were more apparent. Eventually the rim of the container touched the man's lips. They would not open; the man summoned all his power to keep them shut. Strength, however, was soon in league with the entity, and his mouth was forced open. The liquid flowed in and was taken noiselessly down. The man couldn't spit it out as his resolve was spent in resistance before that point. His arm dropped, heavily whacking the counter as his hand released the cup. In an instant it had vanished into the hungry wall.

The entity expected the man to be subdued in short order: it had only to wait. The man, trying to gather himself, crossed his legs and eased into a sitting position. He vaguely suspected what was in motion, could feel changes taking effect. The world about him was less sharp, his sense of being not so acute, his emotions fading gradually. The cloak of darkness advanced sepulchrally.

And suddenly the man rose, surprising all that was part of him. He found he could still put up a fuss, though it was excruciatingly more difficult. Reacquainting himself quickly with his failing knowledge of the room he occupied, the man forced his uncooperative body behind the counter. The glass vessels were blurred in eyes that looked straight at them. The man found the one he had tried earlier and blew across it once more, with no good result.

His minded greatly foggy and muddled, the man took the tall glass and made for the door. Out in the surrounding yard he stopped with a jerk and pulled the object to his mouth. Finally the note was struck, and it resonated throughout the woods. The sound would work, he could cause it when he wanted. The man knew he was the victim of a lie.

CHAPTER SEVEN

It was the middle of the next day, just after lunch. The man was walking along somberly, with the glass from the pharmacy held at his side. He had forgotten what it was or how he had acquired it. Indeed, he only barely realized it was there. The entity inside the man assumed the object would be thoughtlessly left somewhere and was concerned that hadn't happened yet. The sun shone happily over the man's shoulder, on this back to the ordinary day.

The man never had any difficulties about the sun. If he was walking into it his eyes adjusted precisely, his pupils at times not much larger than a pinhead. The amount of light allowed through at any given time was more than enough for him to see comfortably, and little enough to prevent damage to the lens. Sunburn was not a threat: the man's skin had been conditioned to resist the ultraviolet light, and had easily passed its recent test. The man's complexion was golden on the day of his creation, and would stay just that way.

As he walked he only half noticed what was around him. He skirted the edge of a rather large lake, and this gave him pause; that which was not him wasn't totally successful. But no coherent thoughts had developed, and the man left the lake behind without question. Other than that all he encountered were trees, generally in small clumps, and some tall grasses. The landscape was a redundancy, picking up a rhythm which could have been fascinating and comfortable, but was instead dull and mindless.

But then a large patch of wildflowers stealthily crept over the forward horizon. In this chess match wherein the participants defended the same king, the first unexpected move had been made. The entity within knew what was supposed to lie along the man's current route: it could not know what had, left alone, changed over time. Still, changes in landscape weren't supposed to affect him. Yet there are loopholes in every contract, and Nature was a sharp and prudent lawyer. She would take advantage of every one.

The flora had reclaimed the area with a spectacular resolve. A stunning array of colors leapt forth to the man, the sun brightening them all the more as its rays were zealously taken in by the plants. Virtually the entire spectrum was represented. Vivid reds shared the field with luscious blues and delightful violets. Orange and yellow blooms sat with queenly aura on deep green stems. It was like nothing the man had ever seen. The collars on the other uniforms were only remotely comparable. They were merely present on a suit: these colors were alive. The field offered an example of degeneration far beyond that of the apple orchard from many days ago. A void had arose in the manicured vegetation, and older forms of plant life were happy to fill it. By the time the entity realized what was coming it was too late. The man walked directly into the mess: the flowers commanded attention. His line was broken as he began to wander the field.

He was drawn first to a kind of rosebush. Though not particularly tall it was grown enough that its branches had started to turn toward the ground. The blooms were dark red, really almost maroon. There was a multitude of them, contrasting with but nicely complimenting their green support rods. The blooms were not exactly as roses: the petals were odd shaped, like tiny maple leaves, and there were fewer of them than on a traditional rose flower. So, then, the area was not composed of the flora of the man's primitive ancestors. These apparently older flowers were were actually from the interim, between the here and now and the time before the refinement process began. New plants had been bred and their seeds sown worldwide in a period when such trivialities were believed important. Priorities do change, however, and the revised vegetation had been thought eliminated. Yet they had only gone dormant, to return when the pesticides broke down.

The man approached the bush and reached to touch one of the blooms. Gingerly he took a petal between his thumb and forefinger. It was very soft, and very smooth. The man studied the wispy veins in network within. He then tried to snap it off. It would not yield; the petal seemed fused to the rest of the bloom. He then attempted to break off the entire flower, and was sharply rebuked by a thorn protecting its turf. The scratch stung only for the instant before the man's antibiotics went on the offensive.

A thought was placed in his mind that the plant life was deceitful, calling him on only to hurt him. The idea lingered for a moment, and the man did begin to distrust his discovery. It was then that he noticed the aroma of the roses. The smell was sweet enough to taste: a curious thing in itself. Initially he wasn't sure where it came from. Finally leaning his nose into the bloom, the man realized the source of the pleasure as the aroma became stronger and sweeter. He inhaled deeply, allowing the fragrance to spread throughout his person. He had acquired a new memory.

The man elected to take a bloom with him. But not the one he held. He chose another on the presumption it would do no harm. Grasping the stem behind another bloom, he immediately felt the sharp points of the thorns. The man released the thing quickly, and while he had not gripped it tight enough to break his skin a hurt had been caused. The man tried several other flowers yet he always found the thorns. Apparently he would not be able to take any of the roses.

A paradox struck the man. He liked the appearance of the flowers, and was delighted by their fragrance. Yet they hurt him. He experienced a goodness and it rebuked him, and such left him confused. The entity would play on this concept.

"Such things are not necessarily what they seem. What looks to be good may only be to hide a hideous truth. The flowers look nice, smell nice, and feel nice. But their reality is pain. What grand trickery, what an evil scheme! The falsehood they represent is the falsehood of all the untamed world. The eyes see so that curiosity may develop. The unregulated senses pull one into a trap, the bait made juicier by touch, taste, and smell. All so that the trick can cut deeper. Suddenly the trap springs, and pain erupts into the only truth, pain mental nearly as much as physical. Men are thus played for fools, caught in eternal torment."

It was tempting to think like that. On the surface the argument was logical. The roses could be part of an elaborate ruse, a single ploy in a game designed for the warped pleasure of a spiteful and wicked master. He may be nothing more than a lab rat under the spell of a supreme sadist waiting for innocent misery.

Perhaps. But the problem for the entity was that the man had to think the point out. It had to rely on his judgment as much as any potential master did. The man could be given data from both the entity and the surging natural world, and there were few instances when the latter failed to give him something to ponder. The more to consider, the longer until a decision. The more time the process took, the less apt the man was to side with his mentor.

For the time being the man would just leave the red flowers alone. Because he did not understand why they were as they were the man figured it best to postpone any final thought on the matter. Besides, he wanted to examine the rest of the area. So he did the easy thing: he procrastinated. At times the man was more human than others.

Just beyond the roses were a clump of violet flowers arranged over several stems, a dozen blooms per stem. Each stem grew out from the ground to a height of two feet. Five petals sprang from a yellow center on every bloom. The blooms were small, barely an inch in diameter, and quite flat. They ran up the stems in pairs, one to the right and another to the left in tandem. At the very end of the plants the stems turned sharply downward, not like the roses which were bending due to their weight but because that was the way they were supposed to be. The effect was that the end blooms hung inverted, umbrellas for non-existent ants.

Although different, the purple flowers had qualities similar to the red. Their aroma was fainter and not as sweet but pleasing nonetheless. The man took one bloom and held it close to his nose for a sniff. An itch began to grow in his nostrils. It developed quickly and harshly and threatened a sneeze, but such was averted when the man rubbed his nose theatrically. A speck of the yellow core had lodged itself against a wall of his nose, teasing for a moment before it was removed.

Despite the treatment he had received the man was smitten by the blooms, and decided to try to take some: if they were willing. Carefully reaching to a spot midway down a stem he was pleased to find nothing of harm. He grasped that stem firmly, intent on pulling it apart. The plant refused assent to this. The man pulled harder while the plant's resistance seemed to increase. He added a twist of his wrist to the effort: it made no difference. Steadily the man added to his pull, irresistible force against immovable object, the plant only just beginning to stretch. Suddenly it gave, the man's arm shooting into the air as a shower of dirt fell about the area. When the dust cleared, he was left holding the plant roots and all.

The man stared at the thing in his hand, then at the rupture in the earth. He went into a squatting position, placing his hand in the shallow hole and running it slowly through the cold soil. Other plants in the cluster had been pulled up slightly, and a few had been flung well away by the force of the extraction. The newly exposed dirt was soft, a rich black dirt which filtered easily between the man's fingers. He grabbed a handful and shook it, watching intently as it returned almost smokelike to the ground. Toward the surface the dirt was a drier, chunky gray. The man broke up many of the chunks, leaving them as powder.

His attention turned to the stalk in his hand. The top was not like the bottom. Above ground level the stem was sleek, a green rod ideal for the support of a fine flower. Below, it was brown-yellow and dirty, bolting incoherently in all directions, each thrust thinner and more fragile until they finally expired. Marbles of earth were held by the twisted grid. The man knocked the bulk of them out, and saw better the maze of crooked lines which appeared to reach down as the green rod reached up. Curious: a world below heading opposite the one above. The man could not then know the hidden workings defined the reality.

He did not want the roots as they weren't as nice as the flowers. But how could the two be separated? The man tried bending the stalk. It curved neatly yet never threatened to break. Up and down, back and forth, angry rotating twists failed to do the job. Then he pushed a thumbnail into the stem just below the last bloom. It cut decisively, juice spurting on the nail as it pushed through. The man allowed the roots to fall into the rupture, and filled it by moving dirt over with his foot. Within a few days they would offer a new plant.

The man studied the liquid left on the back of his hand. It was clear, but sticky (as he realized when he touched it). He put a drop of it on his tongue: the stuff was awful, and he rolled his tongue and lips fervently until his saliva killed the taste. Some of the goo still oozed from the cut in the stem. The man wiped it across his palm, and closed his hand. As he opened it sinews stretched from the base of the palm to the tips of his fingers before snapping. He played that way for a while, closing then opening his hand at varying rates until the ooze began to dry. As he tired of the sport there was nothing left of the game anyhow.

Plant in hand, the man moved on. Then he remembered the glass cylinder. He had set it down next to the rosebush and now went to retrieve it. There was an echo of an argument against this, but the man didn't notice. Soon the object was back in tow, held opposite the flowers before it occurred to the man he might consolidate his treasures. In a few seconds he had reinvented the vase.

The white garbed earthdweller roamed across the field in no particular fashion. There was plenty to see in such a gaily colored place. Yellow flowers, sort of daisyish, grew around the outer edges of the land. Toward the center was a mass of large bloomed white flowers, giant mums which claimed themselves as the main attraction. Between were day lilies, irises, peonies, even things akin to tulips, an odd match of plants varying from their ancient to reformed styles. Not that it made a difference to the man. He was content to examine them all, forming his preferences according to appearance, fragrance, height, and color. Deeper, richer blooms generally appealed to him over lighter pastels. These latter ones were pretty enough, but simply not what he wanted. The darker blooms held a permanence he didn't see in the others.

The man eventually had picked a small assortment of flowers, rarely more than one bloom of a kind, so that the tall stalk of purple blooms were almost unique in their duplicity. They became more centered in the vase as flowers were added. Soon the purples were surrounded by scarlet and blue flowers. None of the blooms stood taller than the former. The cylinder was filling rapidly.

To the right of the mums sat a patch of Queen Anne's Lace. The blooms were off-white, with lacework wider than any of the flowers the man had collected. The stems holding them up were unusually thin, much more like wire than a rod. The man was impressed by their fragile beauty. He gathered four of them, snipping stems easily with a thumbnail. He placed them in his vase two on each side of the main branch.

The man was now basically satisfied with his floral arrangement. Yet before leaving the area the roses again came to mind. He wanted one, but the memory of his pain delayed him choosing to pick one no matter what. In the end he decided he must have a deep red flower. It took a bit of searching to find the bush, the man's knowledge of its whereabouts skewered by his ramblings through the huge garden. Once he found it he was relieved. But there was still the problem of battling the plant.

Cautiously reaching for a stem, the man took one between his thumb and forefinger directly in back of a bloom. He eased it to one side: an army of thorns began almost immediately from where the stem was held, marching stoutly and defiantly all the way to the ground. He put a fingertip to the nearest thorn. The intense sharpness of the point was obvious to his purposely gentle touch. The man released the flower to deliberate further.

Then quickly, as if to prevent his changing his own mind, the man took the same stem, this time with one hand directly behind the bloom and the other down the stalk, avoiding every thorn that he could. He assumed bending it would do nothing; he was simply trying to anchor the stem so it could be cut with his right thumbnail. But no amount of pushing would pierce it. Bending the stalk anyway while attempting a cut proved equally futile. The man became frustrated, and that gave birth to anger. He began to bend, pull, and twist as forcibly as he knew. The stem would not surrender. The man then launched into the plant without consideration, grabbing it in both hands and gripping it tight, ignoring the counterattack of the thorns. He bent the stem as hard as he could, harder than he should have been able to, and put his thumbnails opposite each other as a sort of double-edged blade. Finally the first layer of the plant's skin was lanced, and a sticky juice oozed out. The inner layers were fibery, and split individually as the razors went through. And then the man had his quarry in his grasp, a spurt of liquid the signal his cutting was ended.

The man released the stem from his left hand, the thorns slow to leave as they had imbedded themselves in his palm and the insides of his fingers. They popped out virtually one at a time, adding to their coarse punishment as they turned sideways to exit the tiny wounds. Trails of blood formed, and redness overtook the man's palm. He was a little scared at this development, especially as the pain it wrought was allowed to increase as a part of a Pavlovian teaching scheme. He soon wiped the blood off on his pantleg, leaving one large crimson spot and several fading red streaks on his uniform. Small red dots at the base of a series of indentations remained on his hand: the clotting process had quickly capped the injuries.

The rose was still attached to a six inch length of stem. The man removed it from his right hand slowly, only too aware that it would hurt. He felt each thorn leave each wound; he was physically conscious of flowing blood. Not wishing to see the damage the man speedily wiped his hand on his right leg. Then the hurt passed, the blood clotted, and the bloom was his. And that was all that mattered.

The man rolled the flower gently by the stem, nimbly missing the thorns. As it turned the bloom darkened and lightened according to the angle of the sunlight. The dancing shades of red were a joy for the man. Rose fragrance drifted to his nostrils: the flower would have a special place in his arrangement.

As the man bent down on a knee he held the rose like a torch. The deep redness stood out the greater away from any sister blooms. Placing the vase in front of him the man tenderly moved the other flowers until there was an opening front and center. Majestically, the man lowered the rose into place. Then he sat back to admire his handiwork.

The finished product was sort of an uphill climb. From the rose in front the arrangement escalated to the dozen violet blooms. Neatly interspaced were the smaller red and blue flowers. The white lace carried the eyes upward, adding to the stairway effect. Yet in spite of the others the rose was the center of attention. Or, really, because of the others. It was as though there were two circles, one left and one right of center, starting at the rose and moving upward to the last violet bloom before drifting through the lace, coming back around to the point of origin. A constant motion was within the setting. But there was always a pause at the deep red rose.

By the by it was suppertime. From right where he had sat after completing his work the man produced his food packet and ate, hardly taking his eyes off the flowers. He was becoming attached to the blooms he had chosen and put into order. The arrangement was like a pet; when he was finished eating the man bent across to touch the flowers, to sniff at them individually and as a whole. He was pleased and content.

It was time to move on. The man did not resist the idea, but he did take his vase in hand as he left the field. As he walked the movements of the air as stirred by his gait brought a constant fresh aroma to his nose. His mind felt like dancing but his controlled pace kept his body in check. Still, it was one of his more invigorating strolls.

With the twilight came bedtime. The man stretched out on the edge of a grassy knoll near the base of a tree. He placed his flowers directly in front of his eyes an arm's length away. The arrangement was to be his last sight before sleep took over. The soft pride of creativity was on his face.

CHAPTER EIGHT

The next morning the man awoke with great satisfaction. His center-piece greeted him without any loss of quality, the blooms yet fresh and the fragrances yet strong. That this was the man's first sight was unfortunate for the entity inside him. Doubt would automatically be in his mind against whatever it might try to tell him.

The man picked up his vase and began his day. He went past groups of trees, patches of grass similar to plainslands, green woods, stones and occasional boulders, creeks and even a spring. None of it particularly interested him. He wanted something he could add to his creation. The man was studying every bit of landscape as it grew before him, anticipating new flora with each new scene. By noon there were no such pleasant surprises. No matter. Something would arise sometime.

What rose was the wind, increasing gradually over the morning. The two most unique of human companions were entering a section where the air was being cleaned by a harmless breeze not unlike those of summers gone by, but unusual for the time. The wind somewhat dissipated the aroma of the flowers but the man's senses were compensated by the air blowing against and around his body, enveloping him in cool freshness. He could feel his hair teased by the steady movement, lifting then setting down the slight mop on his forehead. He noticed it in particular because his hair normally never left place.

During lunch the man observed that the injuries to his hands were healed, gone without leaving scars. His body was remarkably adept at regeneration where it was necessary. The process was circumvented whenever it would be a bother, such as with the hair or fingernails. The skin and internal organs (except the brain) could reproduce themselves easily and did so often, with no apparent loss of healthy activity or aging. Heart ailments were not a worry, nor were illnesses of the stomach, kidneys, liver, whatever. When a problem was seen on the verge of development the potentially disruptive cells were replaced, shed into the bloodstream where the body's defenses would obliterate them. Not that the cells were partial to disintegration. But the safety system just had to be there.

The man was growing irritated. He had situated himself adjacent to a patch of dry, barren ground. The wind was picking up grains of sand and playfully throwing them at him. Of course, the man didn't realize that. All he knew was sand getting in his eyes, ears, nose, and throat. Some of it even besmirched his flowers. Angrily, sort of vaguely so anyway, he popped quickly up, gathered his things, and returned to his line.

The minor sandstorm was over once the man had covered the hundred yard length of uninhabited ground. He entered a forest densely populated with pines, tall, bristly pines whose greenery did not start until well above the soil. The man stopped to stare up into one, and saw the green thicken until almost nothing else could be seen. The trees, even though they were unleaved, nearly blotted out the sky as they rocketed upward. Just a touch of the closing in sensation came over him; the man took no time in moving ahead.

He left the woods in a relative hurry: his change of pace would have been imperceptible by the eye. At his exit the man stepped onto an actual footpath, one of the few which coincided with his direction. There was in fact an extended system of foot highways, each covered with a clear sheet of hardened material. The one the man now walked upon jutted at an exact right angle off another which ran against the back of the forest he had emerged from. All paths were straight as dies. There were no curves or turns, only right angled intersections.

The footways were laid out for best use, connecting the most important areas for access in the shortest amount of time. They were needless to say for the inferior members of the species; the man had no need of them, they merely occasionally aligned with him. The only curved passages were the waterways, because that could sometimes improve their flow. The reason for the penchant for sharp angles on the roads was long forgotten.

Along the path were heavy bushes, thick leaved plants four feet high and tightly packed so that there appeared to be but two long bushes, one to each side of the path for as long as it ran. Short trees twenty feet apart were set at the back of the foliage, which was twenty-five feet deep. The trees were ten feet high themselves, with densely packed branches immediately atop the bushes. The tree leaves were a standard green, while those of the bushes were very dark, nearly black. Beyond the sides of the path were taller trees, short and long grasses in planned alternation, and sparse middling vegetation. It made a relaxed background for the scene.

The passageway was truly regal. The blue of the sky, the brown of the earth under its clear and sturdy protector, the bold green lines of plant life together created an unprecedented splendor. The man became aware of the gravity of his surroundings and stealthily corrected his gait to correspond to it. As the bushes rolled in the breeze, which felt to be heading straight into him, another magnificence was added. The waves made the bushes pleasant, their soft ripples poetry in motion. The lowest branches of the trees lifted gently, granting better glimpses of the beyond. The path was a model of symmetry, it and its siblings the last conscious works for sheer aesthetic value.

The man strode down the path looking very much the monarch. With the corners of his vision he caught the wonder of the dancing foliage. Suddenly something flashed, ahead and to his right. Initially it registered only slightly, but with a quick jump the object verified itself. It was coming closer to the man, faster than what he was headed towards it. As it drew nearer he heard a crackling sound apparently caused by the thing. By the time it was about even with him the man decided he had to have it. Setting his flowers at the path's edge he forced his way through the bushes, which resumed their places once he was past. His calculations accidently correct, the man was able to meet the object as it leapt from a hiding place. He shot out his right arm and snatched it, inadvertently crumpling it into a ball. It was only a piece of paper, one of the things being cleared from the area. The paper had fantastically remained undetected and unharmed for many years.

The man retraced his steps exactly, retrieved his vase, and continued along the path. He was rather enjoying his walk and figured to examine his discovery later. Held tight, there was no danger of it leaving him.

It was late in the afternoon when the man sat to unfold the paper. He was very careful in his work; the paper began to rip at one point so that he became all the more particular. When it was completely unfurled he saw the writing which was on the one side, but gave it little thought. The man turned the paper over, then moved his head slowly back. He was staring into the eyes of a tall blond woman.

She was a very good looking woman as he was a very good looking man. Not stunning, not gorgeous, simply the average woman perfected, striking because of her hair, which was a sharp yellow, and her eyes, a wonderfully precise blue pair. The man sat, laid the picture on the path, and ran his hand firmly over it, trying to get out the wrinkles. The woman was clothed in a white uniform like his, but with an orange collar. The paper itself was a proportionality brief, the writing on the back explaining the success on the front. She was the ideal proportion: no more could be done for the her.

The man meticulously studied the figure on the paper. He concluded that whatever it was was like him, but could see obvious differences in comparison with his memory of his own image. The woman stood sideways, her arms relaxed from her body. She was more rounded in the hips than he, thinner at the waist and in general, and the man looked down at himself to verify the difference in their chests. Her head was more oval than his, her skin golden yet not as rich in color, her hair straight and shoulder length with precise bangs across the forehead. A slight, pleasant smile curved her lips.

Her eyes held the man spellbound. They looked back at him as nothing else could have, not even as his earlier reflection. Her gaze was heavy and robotic yet something else fought through, a faint echo of warmth and compassion. The woman, although merely a picture, gazed upon him as if she understood his situation. The man had more in common with her than he could have known. There would be no yellow collared women.

The female form had reached its zenith and nothing more could be done for it. The body had been made super-efficient in all its functions; in exterior it matched the highest computer standards. But the male body did everything better, whether in the precision of heart rate or the contest of a run. As human bodies were improved all activities became easier, but they became easier faster with the male. The technology was to concentrate on that form. What women still lived were allowed to complete life, not because of the dignity of so doing as to monitor their decay in the hope of finding clues to further the refinement of the male. They were well-controlled beings, the last of the females, always obediently reporting to the medical labs as time and necessity demanded. Warned of impending death, each aided in their own disposal. They reported to special places where they could die in a sanitary fashion, where their bodies could be studied further before their destruction.

Women had, of their own free will, given up their essence in advance of their demise. The one on the paper was a shell, a fine sight but without substance. She had a womb but could become pregnant only with the implantation of a fertilized egg: she produced no ova of her own. The man lacked reproductive power as well; individuals could not be trusted with the future of the species.

Under the guise of reproductive freedom women were sold into reproductive tyranny. Told the choice was theirs, it happened that if they did not have children, someone else would, and did. The female body became little more than a tool. Motherhood was abandoned, and with it a woman's best claim to history, an entitlement far above what any man could aspire towards. Isolated to her own generation the most a woman could generally influence is that single era. As a mother she affects many, not merely by births but by the moulding of an individual. Mothers are remembered and cherished by the force of that fact. The uttermost writer, doctor, or educator, once gone, can be brought to life only through the unreliable industry of others. Mothers touch on the very core of our selves, and are more personal than any historical figure or ideological movement.

Whence comes our humanity. As it were, control over the human race moved from a living, thinking, empathetic being, into the snowballing force of a sterile idealism.

The downfall of woman was caused by a savage egotism, driven by a few and easily taken advantage by the forerunners of who came to rule the world. They believed a woman couldn't be a woman until she was more like a man. She was somehow inferior if she were not. It was a false morality; the question of inferiority never belonged in the discussion. The crux of the problem lay in the egotist's refusal to accept that there were any differences of any kind between man and woman. The fact of the differences was labelled a sign of a man-inspired male superiority. And if perchance such was the case, if it could be changed so that the male had died first, would it really be important?

Man and woman were not simply different in physique but in spirit and temperament. The feminine looks inward and demands honesty, particularly of one's own motives and actions. The masculine looks outward and demands justice, that things should be as they ought to be. They stand astride: if one falls the other falls with it. In this history men and women went into competition in place of working for their mutual benefit. If women didn't have to have children men didn't have to support them. With the door to potential family closed the need of self-sacrifice died. A selfishness ensued which led mankind from certainty to belief to opinion to apathy about fundamental obligations. Traditional society ceased to be, and the vacuum created ballooned maniacally.

What remained was a picture on a paper held by a being barely more than a three dimensional picture himself. If it weren't for the obvious clues, the uniform, the arms and legs, and especially those eyes, the man would never have suspected anything in common with himself. Yet that was enough to plant the seeds of longing in him.

Dinnertime arrived. The man had to force himself to heed the order to eat, not that he was in revolt that second, simply that he was in a type of shock. He had never considered the chance of beings like him having been at any time extant. He sat the picture down, and it was nearly taken by the breeze. He put the vase on the top right corner of it, then placed his knee on the opposite angle. He gazed into the woman's eyes, and noticed his food less than ever.

Afterwards came the problem of how to store the gift. He started to crumple the paper but stopped after the vague thought that it would be somehow indecent. There were no pockets on his outfit save where he kept his food packet, and the man was not fond of having her there. He strode a little way down the path simply holding the paper by a corner, but grew afraid the wind might rip it from his hand. Finally he wrapped the paper around the stem of the vase, picture side in.

The man came to an intersection, the crossing road identical to what he had just travelled. The low foliage and the precisely spaced trees across the back of the route blocked his way. He plowed straight through them, and proceeded across a large field of flat grass which seemed painted to the ground. About a half-mile ahead was a group of trees. His line would intersect them slightly to one side.

The man sat at the edge of the small wood and unrolled his picture. He looked deep into the woman's eyes; they could control him so easily.

It was an effort to put the paper down, but sleep approached so that he had no choice. Carefully the man re-rolled it around the stem, so that her face was the last thing he saw.

Overnight the wind remained, increasing its tempo from time to time not in gusts but by gradual ups and downs. From where the man slept it was able to whip around the little forest, the circular route granting the breeze a greater effect. It began to snatch at the paper, unravelling it to expose the head of the woman, then causing the picture to spin slowly around the vase, each rotation steadily loosening the wraps of paper. Suddenly it was yanked from its holder, as if taken by the top and pulled. Quickly the paper was whisked away, fluttering and waving in the wind, the woman stealing a glance at her sleeping companion before she was blown completely from sight.

CHAPTER NINE

The next morning the man awoke without noticing much of anything. He popped breakfast down his throat and waited for word on where to go, content to venture wherever he might be sent. Told to continue his course from yesterday, he began to ascend to a standing position, reaching for his flowers as he did. With genuine horror the man realized the picture was gone. He stupidly turned the vase around, rolling it as though he had merely looked at the wrong spot. The paper's absence confirmed, the man stood in an icy and desperate stillness. He could not move.

Then, frantically, the man dropped to his knees, very nearly upsetting the flowers. He wiped his hands along the ground, running them under the nearest vegetation in the hope of a quick discovery. It was to no avail. The man stopped and searched the line of trees for signs of movement, but the wind had died and there was nothing. The line in the other direction offered only more trees, edging backward out of sight. He jumped up and stared across the field he crossed a night ago. There was but the sun on a bright green plain.

The man tried to determine what to do, but panic kept his mind racing, sending conflicting and illogical thoughts at such a rate that they tended to block one another out. Forcing himself to consider one idea at a time, he elected to explore along the edge of the wood. As he walked he became more calm even though an odd type of fear was settling in.

The man began to think he would not find the woman. Having to accept a loss was that strange fear.

He followed the line of trees, vigilant towards the landscape as he went. The man didn't realize the line curved and was the second time around before seeing he had gone in a circle. There had been absolutely no motion in the surrounding fields. He was falling into despair, particularly after forays between the trees produced no good result. Yet the promise of another moment kept him glancing over and digging under foliage: the woman may be trapped somewhere close, perhaps just beyond the next tree. Criss-crossing through the forest granted no acceptable discoveries. After he had spent the bulk of the morning on the hunt the man knew he was no better off than when he started. He sat down and glared ahead, seeing the nothing he expected.

The man's young heart was broken. He experienced that emptiness in the stomach which at the same time felt like a tremendous ball. It seemed always to grow, even when there was no possible room left to expand. The anguish was constantly magnified, a pain much worse than anything the man had experienced physically. He had no idea how to handle himself. He wanted to get up and run, stay planted to the ground, even to throw something, all at once. It occurred to the man that he might work his way back across the field, but it was an idea quickly abandoned. It was pointless; she was gone, and her absence was irrevocable.

The entity within kept silent. Although it was in a certain sense of the word pleased with the loss of the paper it knew that in his current state the man was volatile. Caution was called for. What the entity really wanted was to cause a dilemma for its host, then at the precise time offer a resolution he could not refuse. It wished to force the man into the mistake which swallowed his ancestors: a security that would free him of pain and want.

To that end the thing which was not him sent untraceable, warring thoughts and emotions through the man. This caused him to want, instantaneously, to continue his search in the vain hope of finding the woman and to abandon it, not that she could not be found but was not in fact worth finding. The pros and cons rushed lightning fast across his mind. Emotions—deep sorrow at his loss coupled with an inexplicable relief the paper was no longer a burden, self-pity lacing into anger at her as if she had left of a will, anger at himself for not guarding her more closely along with an arrogance toward the woman as inferior any-way—alternately crashed together and pulled at his innards. It was these harsh conflicts clambering for attention which were supposed to draw the man into the trap.

But the plan would not work so readily. As the man sat in torment the torment itself eventually blended into an amorphous unit. This muted its effect, until the man grew into a sense of ease, a sort of cold rationality. The why of recent events now plagued the man, more so than the anxiety they created. He had to know the reason behind them. This urge became stronger as he sat. He no longer sought a solution to his problems: he wanted answers to his questions.

So he raised himself up and progressed through the woods in short order. The redundant landscape passed without his care. The area was well cultivated, a series of tiny forests and sharply manicured lawns. From once the man set foot on the prim and proper aisleway of the day before he was destined to a place of earthen symmetry. The forests were identical, spaced evenly on the grass fields, islands in a sea of college green. Though not as regal as the walkway the land still carried a hint of nobility.

Soon there came in the distance the tops of buildings, brilliantly white in the sun. They were beyond a line of vegetation which was the back of another groomed footpath. As he approached it the man noticed the compound was different from those he was used to. The structures were larger, and there were two rows of them behind the first set all the way around. The man plowed through the bushes and onto the clear walk, taking it to the main white aisle of the compound. He stepped onto it because it was there.

What the man was visiting amounted to a city. It could accommodate five thousand people in the days of old. The buildings out from the main one were mostly bath houses, bunk houses, and food stations. A clinic and a drug outlet were somewhere as well. The whole place might be likened to a resort. It was a spot where the lesser souls could congregate. It was what community had become.

Underdeveloped men insisted on having places to go. They were not content simply being able to move about as they pleased: even the few genuine drifters always wanted a general direction for which to head. Further, despite all basic physical needs having been relieved there was still the social animal to be satisfied. The mental assistance of relationships between the selves was a bane of the lower forms. Thus communities as this were constructed, false fronts which shallow men believed allowed them comraderie within independence. They were wrong on both counts.

The man moved slowly down the central path. He was a little in awe of his surroundings. All the buildings seemed to tower above him; he had never seen anything more than ones with ground floors. There were a couple of pavilions large enough to handle the greater number of people expected in such a compound. They had many rows of high-backed seats: it was nothing but a concession, humoring the egos of those who made mountains out of the comfort of their sitting.

If the man had bothered to check one of the compound's bunk houses he would have found three floors of identical cubicles, each with a rectangular flat protruding from the right hand wall. They were the property of no one in particular, and reservations weren't necessary. When someone new arrived they searched until an unoccupied room was found, slept until refreshed, and perhaps chose a new one if they stayed for an extended period of knocking around the pseudo-city. Freedom, this time of choice, was delighted in. Occasionally an obstinate fellow would stake a claim to the exclusive use of a certain cubicle. Ultimately such statements were silly and futile.

But he wasn't interested in any of that. He made straight for the door in the center of the main structure, situated typically at the end of the widest part of the path. The door slid open gracefully as his approach ended. A warning was issued that he should not enter. It was all the invitation the man needed.

Immediately inside was a large room, well lit and sparsely furnished. At the center back was a doorway, beyond which was blackness. It was the start of a walkway that ran deep into the building, which was itself tremendously long. The man proceeded to the opening, and stood peering into the darkness. Finally, in spite of considerable reservation, he stepped into the passage.

The man walked well into the corridor without event, before noticing that it stayed bright enough to keep his pace regardless of the distance he had covered. This gave him pause; he remembered how dark the walkway had appeared from the main room. He turned his head slowly, then allowed his body to follow. Far behind him was a tiny circle of light, the only hint of the lobby. Between the man and that light it was black as coal.

His initial reaction was to go back. The man fought the urge: the unknown held a certain appeal, and he wondered perhaps if that would wane with discovery. Then, too, he was puzzled at the light which was with him. It consisted of a ring which ran around the floor, walls, and ceiling, brightest where he stood and fading out a few feet forward and back. Whether he stepped ahead or behind the ring kept with him, illuminating the same area. He leaned to one wall: it was not warm, and the light seemed no more intense. Indeed, it was actually dimmer, though he couldn't tell from his proximity. The force of the light changed for the comfort of his eyes.

The man straightened himself. There wasn't much to do save finish his journey. His was a slow, measured stride now, allowing him to actually see the borders of the ring move. Gradually he increased his rate, and the circle of light matched it precisely. Stopping occasionally, he found the light stopped almost before he did. It always covered the same amount of space, reaching just far enough in both directions to permit a comfortable jaunt regardless of speed. The man proceeded steadily, until his attention was caught by a ray of white in the distance which shot across the passage.

It was definitely a crossing beam rather than the end of the corridor. The man was drawn to it, gently prodded down the hall. His movement was nearly involuntary, although not caused by the entity inside him. It did not want him venturing further, but could not prevent him. Within moments the man was at the ray.

He stopped to observe the light across the path. He could just about see the individual rays. Moving to block them he was greeted by his shadow, more apparent than ever against the stark whiteness of the far wall. After a brief reacquaintance the man turned to face directly into the light. There was a short corridor leading into a small room in which a television screen was imbedded in white atop a tiny platform, centered to the corridor. The man entered the room, which lit up softly, surely, and quietly on his crossing the threshold.

There were actually three terminals, one to each side of the one visible from the main passage. All were planted in the same white casing, offshoots from the walls as was everything else. On each screen random bits of information were flashing. They would appear for just long enough for easy reading before fading out gracefully. This was what they did whenever there was no specific information requested. The man eased close to the center screen and watched the changing figures. He could read the flashings, having been trained in the language which would be as a foreign tongue to the ancients. What currently appeared on the screen was no matter to him.

The man's mind began to wander. He was thinking over recent events in his life, back to the first things he could recall. In his mind's eye he was at the stream taking that next drink of water, the one which had been forbidden. The water was cold and delightful. The fellow in the daydream was, shall we say, drowned in the thought. As the man dreamt a question formed in his subconscious. He wanted to know what the water was. At the point when the question was psychically enunciated, something odd happened. The screen in front of the man went blank, the crapshot of images ripped from it.

It was several seconds before the man realized what had occurred. The instant he did the screen resumed its parade of data. He watched the items severely now as they changed, looking for other irregular beats. But the renewed pace was steady, and soon the man drifted again. He was in the apple orchard, and a gentle wind moved through the trees. An apple hung in front of him. He took it, and ate heartily. It was a sweet and sensual experience. The man half wondered what the fruit was, that it could please him so well.

The screen went blank a second time.

The man broke his reverie, and immediately the screen restarted. He was then very suspicious of the interruptions in the flow of information. He decided to set a trap. He watched closely as the screen continued spitting things out, while carefully controlling his own thoughts. The memory of the woman came forward. He remembered her hair, her slightly parted lips, those captivating eyes. The man missed her terribly, and almost fell to his sorrow. But he was able to control himself enough to note the varying forms on the terminal. And then, although it was impossible for him to actually put it into words, the man captured the essence of a question. He asked the screen: Who was on the paper?

As the man stared intently, the writings vanished.

By the time the screen returned to normal the man had already pulled himself away. He was convinced select information was deliberately kept from him, and he took affront at the idea. The man wanted to know what, and why, although not really by whom, because he had no significant grasp of diversity of being. He vaguely believed he had a right to know, a correct enough assertion despite its childish origin. He was thoroughly peeved.

Backing out of the room, the man turned to face the initial corridor. His equilibrium was off, and he forgot the direction from which he came. He elected to go to the right, for no other reason than he felt like it. Either way, perhaps there may be an answer somewhere in the place.

The circle of light was quickly and efficiently upon him. The man walked for a very long time without comprehending the distance, to suddenly find his path blocked. Such an abrupt end of the line startled him, and the man stepped backwards. It was a door, the facing of it a different texture from the walls and ceiling, with the hint of a frame. That was quite unusual: the man had never seen the likes of one. And he had never been refused entry before either. He stared incredulously at the thing in front of him. This was more of an insult than the terminals going out. It may be that he couldn't control the screens, but he had every right to get by that door. Or so the human animal thought.

The man threw his body against it but the door would not budge. Slamming into it several more times also made no impression. He then flattened his palms on the door, tucked his head between his shoulders, anchored his legs, and slowly increased a push until he used every bit of force he had. The barrier remained impervious. Panting inaudibly, the man stepped away to re-examine his adversary. He tried to jam his fingers into the seam of the frame, but it was no good. The wall material did give slightly, but the frame held fast. The man was just not going to get by.

Total frustration enveloped the man. He was now positive the answers he sought were available, but not to him. He launched one last futile slam on the door, more for the satisfaction of it than in the hope of actually breaking through. For several moments the man stayed against the blockage, before rolling around and sliding to the floor.

In the distance were faint rays of light from the small room. The man looked upon them only because nothing else could be seen. His chest was heaving though his breathing was still unheard. There seemed nothing to do but leave. Resolving himself to that, the man rose and started the retreat.

He was much more abrasive in his gait now that he was acclimated to the surroundings, and because of his anger. The man stopped briefly at the place with the terminals, but left them quickly in disgust. A dot of light soon shone, tiny but growing constantly, and then he was back in the lobby.

The man went to a side bench and sat down hard. He considered the role he felt to be playing: the servant to some untraceable ideal. His dislike for the part was fermenting. But what could he do? One cannot fight what cannot be seen, let alone that the invisible force writes the rules of conduct as it so willed. And this in fact was what the man was in contention with: a vague will which could retreat and regroup easily in the face of adversity. It was as a jelly: no form save its container. The man was that vessel.

There was a heaviness in the man's stomach similar to what he felt at first losing the woman, but worse due to his latest discoveries. He felt profound anguish, and a general unbounded helplessness. Not wanting to face such a reality and seeing no reason to just sit, the man started to leave the building. He intended to leave the compound well behind as quickly as possible. Yet before he could effect his plans it was suggested he replenish his food supply. Why not? The structure to the right of his exit was a food station.

The man entered the depot. There was no downward ramp, only lines and slots on the walls of the single room. Randomness sent him to the center of the back wall. An instant before he reached the chosen slot a little parcel popped out and waited on the narrow counter. The man looked at it with no reaction.

Then, in a rush of inspiration, the man though of what he could do. He would refuse the food packet: in fact, he'd leave the remains of his current supply on the counter beside the new stuff. He did not need it: if he wasn't good enough to be told certain things he was not good enough to eat the food. He would, he should, go where he wanted when he wanted. No object which would not show itself could tell him what to do.

It was a fateful decision, greeted with the utmost alarm. The great experiment was in peril beyond the worst possible belief. The declaration by the man was the first salvo in the coming struggle. The final world war had begun.

CHAPTER TEN

It was the middle of the next morning. The man had missed three meals and would soon miss a fourth, but appeared no worse for the wear. The terrain had not changed from recent days: flat grasslands interrupted periodically by groves of trees. The man had left the compound at a truly random angle, and was heading in a northerly direction. There was a proud and distinguished look about him today, in the first throes of independence, even considering the uncertainty the man felt about his chances. He was more or less happy at the turn of events, so that he did not completely notice the discomfort in his stomach.

The man was developing into a conspiracy theorist, not without some justification. He saw through quite a number of things, believing for example that whatever was keeping information from him was somehow responsible for taking the woman away. The voice within him seemed intent on leading him back to the time before he Knew, which meant it could not be trusted and might be part of the program against him. He even suspected something evil about the food. The man's thoughts were essentially of an irrational, vindictive origin, but nonetheless true. And they were a key part of the man he was becoming. With a pioneering spirit he would press on.

The entity inside the man insisted it was foolishness to leave his nutrition behind. The tablets contained all that he needed, expanding with the effect of the stomach's juices to lessen that feeling he was try-ing to ignore, and he could be sure of the supply. These were on the surface reasonable arguments. But the man now had an arrogant edge which refused to weigh the entity's assertions. He was confident the situation would be resolved to his satisfaction.

It is interesting how the man and the entity communicated. Neither could really verbalize but the one always understood the other, at least in the rotest sense. They sort of spoke in concepts, entire trains of thought exchanged in a second or two. It was not telepathy: they occupied the same space. Perhaps it was that nerve impulses had improved as carriers of intent to the point that thought was imbedded in them. Yet that could not account for the abstractions necessary for the transference of ideas. Abstractions are essentially outside of the body, or maybe beyond it, and it doesn't seem possible that they could be carried in physical form. It could simply be that both the man and the parasite were more than they knew. Or the entity was a more dependent creature than its creators would care to acknowledge.

Noontime passed, with the reminder that he should be lunching drowned out. The man decided to take a run. As he sped across the field he observed how his legs pushed and pulled in turn and his arms chugged in unison. He could feel the arm motions helping his body along. The sound of the air as he sliced through it and the breeze in his face were pure joys: the feelings of freedom. Yet it was not wise to burn energy on a hard gallop with the time and contents of his next meal unknown. In this ignorance the man raced ahead, eventually slowing to a jog and then a walk. He did feel refreshed by his efforts.

The man missed his fifth meal as he walked through another patch of forest. He was just a little irritated at the sameness of the trees; they had never been so similar before. He had hoped there would be a greater variety of sights to see. For things to be always exactly alike is paralyzing. The man took a walk around the wood simply because he wanted to, and ended his day.

On waking the next morning he instinctively reached for his food packet. The empty back pocket reminded him of his actions, and the ill-feeling in his belly was more sour. A fairly intense search of the area brought nothing worth consuming. A strained and almost nasty "I told you so" was directed at him. The man ignored this; there were, after all, things to do but eat.

The man left the forest with certainty. The farther he would go, the better off he'd be: or so the man believed. Onward he traversed, increasing his speed as he wanted, slowing his rate when something caught his attention. Most often he kept the inbred pace, which was nothing more than habit now anyway. His eyes were attentive towards possible food, only to come up short for a second day.

The third day found the man tiring, and what had been merely an uncomfortable sensation in his stomach was becoming a true pain. He half-heartedly continued to look for food, no longer really expecting anything to turn up. It was slowly, angrily dawning on the man that his new life wasn't going to be easy, to which the entity was steadily pressing the security argument. He was, you know, still close enough to the compound to go back. The man would hear none of it. He didn't want advice, he wanted good results without delay.

The scenery around the man was changing slightly but definitely, almost meekly. During the morning he had been through an area where the lawns were higher and their colors lighter than in most places. The lighter patches made the grass appear diseased. By early afternoon the shorter, darker grasses were in the minority. The newest grasses weren't very much taller, maybe a couple of inches. Just enough to be noticed if there were no distractions. Such as hunger.

Late in the day came sprouts of particularly tall grass. They were a few feet high and bobbed to and fro gently after an initial harsh movement when the man happened close enough. The sun was off to his left; his shadow a thin line to the right, bouncing off the objects which crept up. The exaggerated shadow lent proof to the slow gait the man now had. Even though his body was super-efficient it was also very dependent on a tightly scheduled, precise diet. As such it would deteriorate rapidly, much faster than an earlier version of his species.

As evening wore on there were other signs that the system which was the external world continued to break down. The grasses were virtually all high, many stalks brown and dry at the tips and closer to the ground. From the underground framework of the forests the first saplings tentatively poked into the surrounding lawns. The trees within the forests were also changing, a little less refined than the ones the man had known before. It was in a group of these where he stopped for the night.

The next morning the man was, naturally enough, hungrier than ever. Knowing that it was important to eat soon, he elected to spend the day combing the wood for food. He searched everywhere, yet found nothing which was to his knowledge edible. There was no option left: it was time for experimentation.

Weary but hopeful the man approached a tree branch which hung at eye level. He intended to try a leaf, for if it were suitable he would have an endless food supply. Looking over the branch as though it mattered which leaf he selected, the man settled for one near the end. Snipping it off cleanly with a thumbnail, he stuck the whole thing into his mouth and began to chew. Almost immediately he spat it out. The leaf had a terrible taste. How could the man know the plants received minerals completely different from what he did, which gave them a peculiar flavor? For a long while the man fought to rid himself of the taste, testing the limits of the contortions his face could make.

Desperation kept the man trying the vegetation. There were leaves on other trees and bushes which just may be different. Then there were the several types of grass. None helped. At one point he resorted to ripping bark off trees, and chewing on stems and branches and stalks of flowers, as well as the blooms themselves as they appeared. He scraped the earth with his fingernails and ingested the small amount of dirt they dredged: that was the worst of all. At day's end he still had nothing safe or satisfying to eat, and his abdomen was hurting. Conceding defeat, the man went to sleep in a patch of tall grass.

The night was not restful. The man had never before moved as he slept: yet he had to now to sleep at all. In the end his rest came in snatches, although he was never quite awake enough to notice anything about his exact status. At dawn a tired and ragged man rose to the world.

He trudged along throughout the day, stopping to rest often. His condition prevented him walking at anywhere near a normal pace, and the terrain did not help. Where plush lawns once had carpeted the fields brush had appeared and thickened at such a rate that even the man took notice. The trees were gathering in larger groups, much more genuine as forests. Short hills popped up which ordinarily would have been crossed easily, yet were mountains to the weakened life plodding atop them. The man pressed on only out of stubbornness. The entity was silent; it believed him too far gone, the two additional days from civilization being about one too many. At dusk the man fell, nearly collapsing, to sleep.

And sleep was again to tease. Tossing and turning, turning and tossing offered no comfort to the man. The hurt in his belly was greater, partly because at night there are no distractions. The entity could have helped him sleep but would not. If the body were, by some chance, to survive the beating it was taking, the man's self was to have a lesson worth remembering.

The next morning came, and the man looked like he should under the circumstances. Grass was on his uniform, but he had to force himself to brush it off. Spots of ground-in dirt graced the arms and legs of the outfit, and he could do nothing with those. A few hairs were uncharacteristically out of place, darting stiffly from the top of his head. His eyes were glazed. It was the sixth day of independence.

The man considered the situation as clearly as he could. Perhaps he was a fool. Perhaps there was nothing for him except mindless allegiance to something which thrived on his ignorance. Yet he could not turn back. He had made his decision and must see it through. That which was not him gave no clues to what was or would happen to him, save to assert he deserved his apparent fate. After years of nurturing and countless hours of care and consideration, he had refused further aid. He had been safe, healthy, and protected yet thought he could do better for himself. So be it. Nature would take her course.

It developed into the longest day of the man's life. The sun felt extraordinarily hot even though it was nothing out of the ordinary, the territory rougher despite his being able to traverse such ground easily in earlier times. He was progressing steadily into a deteriorated land, one that, had the man thought about it, might never even had been developed. It was a wild country, every plant in competition for its parcel of earth. In places the brush was so thick the man could hardly pass.

The trees had jammed nearly into each other in tight packs. The man found it convenient to rest against their trunks: it was easier than lowering himself to the ground. The pain in his midsection had gnawed into numbness, worse than one hurt and spread over his whole being. It would be heavenly if so much as one part of his body were relieved.

The afternoon was slower than the morning. The man was travelling at a rate less than a fourth what he should, covering virtually no ground as the standards went. He began to avoid the more difficult obstacles, going to great lengths to circle them, searching for any break in the foliage before pressing forth. By nightfall he was near defeat. The man fell to earth abruptly when he could go no further. Still he could not sleep: he lay in a stupor.

The man did not move a muscle overnight. Staying still, he grew aware of every part of his body and nothing else. He never actually slept yet was never really awake. All around him was gray, and it seemed as if the agony became more than simply his, that even the space around him was hurting. Throughout the darkest part of night the world was little but the man in his space, hopelessly isolated.

The brightness of the morning finally arrived to clear off the gray. The man could see and know the great blue sky above where he lay, and was, surprisingly to him anyhow, a bit less out of sorts. Still, he did not wish to get up, and was but marginally interested in pressing forward. With a supreme effort of the will he raised himself from the earth, and staggered to the nearest tree. The forest ahead was the thickest yet. But he would get through it, from tree to tree if necessary. He gathered himself the best he could and was off.

It helped that the man held no concept of death. Perhaps then he would have stayed down and waited for the reaper's call. But as he did not know birth, being already alive and at least physically mature when he discovered his senses, he didn't realize life could end. The entity toyed with the idea of explaining this to him, but in its own pride thought he might be reclaimed and didn't want to risk his giving up. So there was little except the man's own pride to make choices, and this led him to continue the adventure. That tomorrow may be different or not there at all was never a consideration. He would get by.

Yet circumstances were on the verge of smothering him. The lack of nourishment and sleep was a venomous combination. The forest had become nearly impassible: rarely was there significant barren ground. Only enough light seeped through the treetops that the man could see clearly. Once or twice he was left groping just the same.

Eventually the man did come upon a small clearing. It was well lit, although a few shadows worked against the light. The man leaned sideways on a tree, preparing for a lumbering dash across the open land. Then he caught sight of a plant to the left of where he stood. It had wrapped itself around the trunk of a tree; hanging from it were many bright red circular objects.

Food; it had to be food. The man associated their color with edibility: it was the kind of association borne of hope and desperation shaped through limited experience. Gathering himself was now an easier chore. Pushing away from the tree harshly and relatively vigorously, he stuttered across to the plant.

The man wasted no effort in snatching one of the objects and shoving it into his mouth. There was no doubt of his discovery. He had found a variation of the tomato, growing wild in a forest which had shed its human captors. Several other vines offered themselves nearby. But the man cared none for them or what they were in particular. What mattered was he could eat them, which he did, one after another. They were not like the apples from earlier in his consciousness, and the man appreciated the difference. There was a certain pleasure in realizing other types of food could be found. He thought, as his hunger faded, of how the new red food was more subtle than the other, and not nearly so sweet. Yet ultimately the important fact was he could eat.

The man ate every tomato on that vine, a dozen or so, before sitting back for a rest. He could almost feel his body rejuvenate. The vitamins and minerals from the new food were not what his body was accustomed to working with yet they were something, and his metabolism as it were could adapt. As his body failed quickly without nourishment, so it could mend quickly even without accurate or refined measurements in his diet. Soon he was able to stand without any extraordinary effort. He was ready to continue his journey, and strode confidently into the forest. There was still an odd sensation in his knees, the residue of his recent weakness. But it soon worked itself out.

Slowly and consistently, the man increased his tempo. His overall appearance had lost something, namely a few pounds, which tied into a lack of muscular quality. He wasn't as well toned and his uniform, in several places, didn't fit quite right. Time would take care of such trivialities.

The man thought he had heard a vaguely familiar sound. At first it was but a low murmur. This grew into a rumbling before giving way to a roar. He was uneasy about the noise the louder it became, particularly as he seemed to be headed directly into it. The closer he approached the more a cloud of violently crashing sound enveloped him. The man was approaching a rise, and once beyond it found himself on the very edge of a river.

He happened upon it so fast and unexpectedly that he almost fell into the raging water. It was a rapids, not actually very rough but appearing wicked to him because he hadn't come across one before. Also, the silence of the forest magnified any sound, particularly those with which the man was unfamiliar. He regained his composure, and stood watching the splashing and bubbling whiteness of the foam as it danced over the peek-a-booing rocks. The man was first in awe, then wonder, then contentment. It was good entertainment.

Obviously a crossing here was ill-advised: it was far too dangerous. Growing bored with the show, the man took a walk along the riverbank. The water calmed itself in its own good time as he ventured downriver. By the middle of the afternoon it was a softly flowing little waterway, and the man could see it was no longer a threat. He turned towards it, and went to the water's edge.

The man saw his image rippling on the water's surface. Even with the distortion he could see the changes in himself. His hair was out of place, his face thinned and gaunt, and there were interesting lines which were gathers in his uniform as it did not quite form to his body. His eyes, too, were not as he remembered.

Settling into a squat, he lowered his hand into the river. It flowed nicely around a weary hand. The man drew water to his mouth, and savored a long drink as a complement to his recent meal. He took another drink, not much, only what he felt he needed. Then he splashed water about his face and neck and hair, rubbing himself vigorously. It was a wonderful feeling, a clean he had never known.

Next, although it was still the afternoon, the man decided to sleep. He backed away from the river, and strolled a short distance until he found an opening in the trees which was the base of a hillock. The man walked carefully up it, yet a bit unsure of himself, and discovered a patch of short grass ideal for laying on. He made himself comfortable, and the sleepiness brought on by food and drink took over quickly.

CHAPTER ELEVEN

Sleep was peaceful. The man stayed totally immobile as his body became as close to fully rested as possible. He awoke neatly recharged. First thoughts were on food, of course. He realized now more than ever the importance of eating. But in looking around the man saw that things weren't right. There wasn't the bright light of daytime, not even so much as the grayness which accompanied the rain. Yet a whiteness dominated the area: it was painted onto things, the leaves of the trees, the rocks along the river, for that matter on the water itself. The scene was eerie: but not necessarily distressing.

The man looked into the sky. Much of it was blocked off by the trees yet he could see enough to notice the tiny, barely flickering points on the deep (very deep) blue background. What might they be? He would need to find a place with a better view. Without a sound, the man crept to the river's edge and walked alongside the quiet water.

The sensation of travelling beneath the twinkling lights was odd. At several points the man had to stop to get his bearings straight: he was the victim of an illusion caused by the trees interacting with the specks of light. It was as though they and not he were moving, and this upset his rhythm. The effect would have ended if the man would simply quit staring above as he walked. But he feared the things would vanish if they weren't kept in sight; he would stick with an awkward gait.

Finally the man reached a significant clearing. To his complete amazement there were thousands of the small lights in the sky, twinkling nicely in succession. The man was entranced by the majesty above him. Only his eyes gave themselves away in movement, steadily gazing over the first night sky they had been treated to.

Eventually the man dropped his gaze and thought again of how white everything on the surface world appeared. He raised his left hand, palm facing him, and watched the whiteness fall upon it as it left the shadow of his face. His shadow: it was very crisply etched on the bare earth in front of him. The man turned around suddenly as if to accuse the night sky of...something. But he was struck dumb at what was there. The fullness of the large moon loomed overhead.

The moon would seem to have grown over time. Disturbances in the atmosphere had been cleared away; what the man saw was not a physically larger satellite but a less obstructed view of the one always present. The lunar face was visible but the man had no way of determining it. He was more interested in the stark whiteness of the object, sharp in spite of the splotches of gray. The man reached upward at the moon, and his hand was framed in brilliance so much so that he almost could not see it.

His face was bathed in white. It became the face of a tragic clown as shadows appeared under his eyes and lower lip. Fear sought influence on the man, not caused by the entity but out of concern for his fate. He considered hiding but didn't know where he might go. He suspected that even in the thickest forest the giant ball would be above, waiting him out, watching for his mistake. Since he had no concept of day and night the man did not expect a return to normalcy. He had but to wait for his destiny.

Yet the mounting of the passing moments began to kill the tension. The man grew easy enough to survey the nocturnal landscape in detail. Reflections of white off the faces of objects contrasted with bold black shadows underneath or alongside; rocks thus appeared two as one. The jet blackness inside the forest was more emphatic in the moonlight. The scene was more like a portrait than real life, with a surreal quality groping and hanging onto all it could grasp. The portrait was given away only by the softly flowing water which bounced the light playfully across the river's surface.

When he became comfortable enough the man sat down. No longer concerned with the single giant light (what else could it be?) the man began observing the stars anew. They sparked and jumped, some bright, some dim, all interesting. As the moon was easier seen the purified atmosphere allowed more stars to show than the ancients knew by the naked eye. The dimmer lights had gained a forum: the man was dumbstruck by the intergalactic display.

By a divine perversity those who had ruled the world had opened the door to a more brilliant natural wonder. The nighttime was more alive than ever. Visibility had been improved threefold: a meteor shower which should have been beyond sight was instead a magnificent show for the pair of eyes which had stumbled across it. A comet raced in solitude across the lower periphery downriver: it was unknown light years out of the solar system. The man sat, contentedly taking them all in.

There were many things which could be done to the terra firma. A flower might be cross-bred to satisfy a fancy, landscape formed into a pleasing geometric pattern, a man carved to fit an ideal. But the deep heavens were unobtainable. On earth she could be bent, twisted, and mangled if the right man desired. But left to her own, she was beauty and grace unmatched. Nature's glory is not necessarily in the alterations so much as the original design.

The man's body was increasingly his own. He awoke in the middle of the night because it was losing obedience to the controlling substances within; firm habits were diminishing as well. He would rise when he was sufficiently rested, not when when a drug wore off or was counteracted; habit died as the man's journey steadily increased the number of days without chemical reinforcement or practical reminders. The checks on his system were either burned away by the last week's actions or overrode by the force of will.

The discovery of tolerable food in the wilds coupled with the rising non-dependency of the safeguards in his metabolism were ominous signs for the entity within the man. A question loomed as to whether the man could any longer be influenced by his masters. A drug which was gone was gone. It was irreplaceable unless the man should ingest more, yet he could not be ordered where to go or what to do via any kind of self-serving logic because he now distrusted the entity. Unpredictability of act and territory compounded the problem. And indications were the man would continue through the unknown area indefinitely.

As he continued to study the night sky the man did not see the plodding changes occurring on his right. Lighter shades of blue crept into the horizon as a ring of scarlet, orange, and gold formed. The trees again partially blocked this effect, but soon enough an open spot allowed the man clear vision. Once the colors were obvious he noted the loss of dominance of the moon and stars. He forgot the night spectacle and turned to watch what the dawn might bring.

It was a slow explosion of daytime, not quite fast enough for the man to really see it happen. Gradually and certainly the collage took over the east. The scarlet overran the other hues until it began pressing its own limits, spreading along and somewhat above the line where earth and sky met. Then, quietly, it was gone, and a streak of piercing white shot into the darkness, casting a halo of brightness towards the man. Streams of sunlight poured into the morning. A tip, then a thin crescent, then a semi-circle advanced into a flaming ball. It was a magnificent finale to the star gazing of the now glowing figure on the water's edge.

He turned his eyes downward as the sun was shining directly into them. Eventually it rose to where the man could look ahead comfortably. The more familiar and less amazing daylight left him to think more about breakfast. Rumblings in his stomach offered another reminder. With a drink and a splash he rose in search of sustenance.

The trees began to encroach on the river enough so there was barely room for passage. The man was often doubled over to avoid low, thick limbs from the squat, gnarled trees of the area. The slight murmur of the flowing water was pleasant, so that the man didn't mind too much his increasing hunger. Having eaten well yesterday allowed him time to forage today. He was not yet in serious need.

As it was, the wait wasn't long. By late morning the man had discovered a tree with yellow, thin-necked, fat-bellied fruits on its branches. They felt like the apples, yet perhaps a little less firm. He took his first bite of a pear and found it to his liking. The man ate steadily, and during the course of the meal developed the habit of tossing the cores into the water; he liked to hear the plunk. Once he was full he grabbed a pair of pears and stuffed them into his pockets while carrying four in his hands. If nothing else he would be sure of dinner.

During the afternoon the entity crept back into the man's mind. It asserted that his travels were adversely affecting the delicate balance of his body. The food he ate was improperly mixed and would, or at least should, not satisfy his appetite or aid his performance in the long run. As it communicated it employed all kinds of abstractions and technical references. But the man could only comprehend on a fairly rote level; he lacked the ability to follow complicated scientific arguments which relied on a solid base of hard knowledge. The entity may as well have been explaining the principles of the extinct gasoline engine. The response of the host organism was not useful. He was impressed by the rattling on of the lecture but unable to verify the claims of the speaker. Consequently, all that was accomplished was a deeper distrust of the entity's position.

The fact of the matter was that his body would learn to digest the new foods. Both for the short term and over time, it could extract and process whatever it needed regardless of the source. Truthfully, though, the entity did not know this. The deceptions involved were so perfect that it believed them itself, so far as it had the ability believe anything. Ignorance and blind obedience were its essence; the entity was as programmed from birth as the man. Really more so: it was a complete creation, while he was at least in part developed from existing material.

The day began winding down. The man was so lost in adventure that he didn't realize the sky was steadily darkening. The sun slipped away behind him: soon the flaming ball was below sight, leaving the barest of a white line beneath the crimson etchings of the evening. It occurred to the man that he was witnessing the inversion of the dawn. He wondered how it was behind him rather than afront. But as he could not solve this problem he chose to simply enjoy the event.

As it had been that morning the changes came too slowly to actually see. The streaks of color narrowed to scratches before fading into the deep blue of night. Stars reappeared, a few initially until it was dark enough for the lesser ones to show. The night was in full force once they began their rythymic and complimentary blinking.

Then the moon rose quietly and regally, only slightly less full than the last nocturne. Her reflections eased forth, tenderly resting on the leaves of the trees and shrubs, the stones on the riverbank, the surface of the water, the lone face which could see it happen. He stretched out upon a patch of short weeds as the moon edged over the center of the river. A single streak of moonlight floated lazily on the soft ripples.

The man's first day then ended.

CHAPTER TWELVE

The man was awakened by an uncomfortable feeling in his lower back. The pears were the source of discomfort, yet happiness welled inside the man once he realized what they offered. Breakfast posed no difficulty this morning.

Dawn had long since passed; only the sunshine greeted him at table. As he ate the man surveyed the landscape. It was rough country yet not impassible. Bushes and shrubs flanked the trees all around, and high grasses and weeds filled in the areas between. The grasses approached the river and stopped abruptly along a shallow, cliff-like ridge which served as a bank. Below the ridge but above the water was dirt and mud and a hint of sand. An occasional root poked out from the cliff wall. The scene was nearly identical on the far shore, the trees encroaching on the water just noticeably more.

The man walked along the river, trying to stay on the grass. At one point he found himself far separated from the rolling water as he had stumbled off into a clearing which ended in a very dense forest. The trees grew so close together that the illumination was merely a grayness, enough to allow free movement yet not much else. The man tried to retrace his steps when he realized the trouble he was in. It was a difficult task in the tight woods, but he finally made it back to the river. From then on it became his habit to stick by the water even if it meant walking in the mud along the bank.

As the man could now know hunger he could also know thirst. He stopped several times for quick drinks. The water was crystal clear, and he could see the brownish riverbed through it. Golden sparkles danced within and upon the bed. The man reached into the current to touch them. His fingers sank deep into the wet sand, and the man pulled out a murky clump of residue. The sand and mud slid off his palm; some fell between his fingers. Tiny gold rocks, little more than pebbles, were left in his hand. They shone but didn't sparkle once they lost the aid of the flowing water. The man rolled them around his hand as though they were marbles. One at a time they dropped into the water, until his hand was empty. He then left them alone; they were interesting, but what good were they?

Before long the man began to consider the possibilities of lunch. Since he had finished his pears he was at the mercy of the land, which thankfully increased in mercy all the time. Soon the man happened across a series of bushes which ranged slightly, from four to five feet high. They were swarmed with berries, black ones and blue, and a good many red. The promise of food emanated from them, and the man was not misled. He started picking and eating them, loving their natural sweetness, and although the colors meant nothing to their taste he concentrated on the reds. They were like raspberries. Broad, flat leaves protected the tiny fruits, so that the man had to hunt underneath them occasionally to continue lunch. Closer inspection would have revealed the plants as having three tiers stacked neatly one atop another, as if they were supported from behind. But details escaped the hungry hunter: he was too busy eating.

The man was unconsciously working his way further downriver, as that was how the bushes ran. In passing he noticed a half-dozen wooden poles sticking out of the water at a point where the berries began to veer away from the river. They were of ancient, rotting wood, shooting a solid eight feet above water level and stained light gray. Any day now they were subject to collapse. The poles were arranged in two rows, three per row heading from the shore into the river. They were in line with a grown over yet obvious path which skittered up a low hill.

The berry plants lined the right side of the path. There was no change in their form, except that the leaves and fruits hung at an angle rather than directly into the earth. Something was definitely holding them up along the hill; their appearance was too deliberate for this not to be. The man was just not astute enough to see it.

When he was finished eating the man turned to get a drink. His hands were stained: no matter how hard he scrubbed the black-red would not wash away. He eventually quit trying, and took his drink. As he raised up he looked straight at the strange things before him in the water, squinting an eye as he pondered what they might be. He walked over and was able to grab one near the river's edge. With only the barest pressure it started to give, yet the man was quick enough to get away from it before either he or it fell. The pole was left with an outward lean; the symmetry of the arrangement had not been perfect anyway.

The man turned around and saw for the first time the trail leading up the hillside. It was an oddity in the middle of a forest. There was no doubt the man would follow it. He walked up the hill astride the berries, popping a few in his mouth as he went. The entity inside him said nothing. It didn't seem to matter this moment what direction he chose.

The grade grew steeper: the incline of the hill was deceptive. Although the man didn't have far to go it seemed to take a long time to get there. Farther along the path the trees began to move in upon it, narrowing the passage considerably. The man started to think the path ended in nowhere, as the forest looked to arc around the trail in a horseshoe. Just ahead of the presumed blockage the berry plants stopped. The man stepped up into a flattened area, expecting to have to retrace his steps. This would not happen, however. The trail led into a cave whose entrance was hidden from the river by the rise of the ground and from the sky by the trees, now so close onto the path that their branches reached across it and intermingled.

The cave mouth was black. Eroded rocks created the frame of the entrance, making it look as though old aluminum foil had been crumpled up and pasted around it. A sprig or two of plant life tried heroically to grow from the rock but with only modest success. The man approached the opening. It was a rough-edged semi-circle, nearly seven feet in radius. With little thought he entered the cave.

The first study the man took of the cave were the crags in the walls, feeling their hardness and uneven texture. Farther into the earth he noticed rocks formed into spires rising from the floor. Several of their cousins hung from the ceiling. Despite the different features of this enclosed world compared to the outside, the man soon grew bored. They, on their own, were basically unchanging. And it was becoming too dark to see; he was prepared to leave when he saw a faint light ahead.

The light was yet far enough away that the man had to take it slow getting there. He touched along the walls to keep his line. Occasionally he feet would strike an object, and the man began to simply shuffle them carefully, so as not to startle himself on an obstacle. Soon the walls and floor started to flatten, and the man realized that nothing further protruded into his path. Then he arrived at the light, which was behind a cone that pointed upward, giving a clamshell effect on the wall above. The light was one of many which lined a corridor. The corridor veered noticeably to the right, with the lamps at regular intervals on each cave wall. The man dutifully followed the path along.

The walls were still uneven if no longer jagged. They were streaked, and often blotched, gray, white, and brown. After he had walked a fair distance in the finished section of the cave the man's feet began to hurt. They were not accustomed to the surface of the remarkably smooth floor. The precisely spaced lines would have given it away to anyone who could have known. The floor was concrete.

Next, and to his growing disappointment (he now liked the explore after the change in appearance) the man thought the cave was coming to a dead end: it stopped about a hundred yards ahead. Nevertheless he pressed on, finishing his trek under the hill as a climber inversely completes the ascent of Everest. But the way wasn't actually blocked. Centered to the walkway and cased in a sturdy frame was a gray steel door, with a silver handle on the middle right. The handle was too much of an invitation to be left alone. The man grasped it firmly and pulled. The door squeaked as it opened, and he had to pull harder to swing it out from the frame. The man looked beyond the door, perplexed at the sight.

It was a finished room thirty feet square. Along each wall were ceiling to floor bookshelves, stocked full. The shelves were a light stained wood, possibly pine, and simple in style, upright rectangles crossed by unevenly spaced planks; shelf heights varied because book heights did as well. Florescent lights shone from above a dropped ceiling which was otherwise white, in two by four foot sections. In the center of the room sat a large table made of heavy wood, with several chairs of the same wood stationed around it. The furnishings were stained to match the shelves. In a far corner on its own stand was a single large book.

Long before, when the fate of mankind was in place beyond reversal, a tiny cadre of men and women in a last dying gasp had carved this hole in the earth and stuffed it with the arts, history, science, philosophy, and theology. The great books were all there: at least, as many as industry and luck had allowed. They were placed in the room to create an archive in the hope that somebody someday would find it and use it. During the time of the builders the room was a place of discussions fruitful to the soul. It was not possible to have them anywhere else.

What the few had done was set up their own school. The academies of their day were useless, even contemptible. Not a question could be answered; indeed, few thoughtful ones arose. The dead spoke more powerfully and truthfully than the living, only to be shut up and derided by teachers who had no real comprehension of their subjects. Education had become socially relevant, and therefore transient. Those at the head of the classrooms spewed propaganda according to circumstances in flux, and students lost sight of their positions relative to other generations.

The continuum of History was broken. Detached peoples became lost in their self-importance. Eventually a force, developed by man ostensibly for the benefit of mankind, had come to the fore. It goaded the pride of individuals towards unconditional surrender to it, and when that happened to a significant majority the past was erased and the future written before its time. One generation changed man absolutely.

The man stood in total amazement in the doorway, his right hand still holding the handle. The founders had been able to erect and keep hidden a power system which kept the lights going and provided electricity for other uses. The man was impressed by the different type of illumination: it wasn't as pure as what he knew. The full shelves and obscure furniture also had their effect; they aroused not suspicion but curiosity. As the sense of awe lessened the man allowed himself to enter the library. The door closed gently behind him.

He took a slow, methodical tour of the room, running his fingers over the book bindings lightly as he passed. Pausing at the large tome set off to itself the man traced the ornate carvings on the cover with his pointer. Next he admired the superior finish of the table top. He easily found the impurities as he rubbed his right palm across it, but was pleased about the object just the same. The man discovered that the chairs moved; they were medium backed with three square rungs and broad, formed seats. He pulled one out and sat in it, thinking. He was unsure what to do.

It had not occurred to the man that a book could be removed from a shelf. He assumed each shelf was one large unit with each text welded to its neighbor. Before he could experiment, though, he saw there was another door, a wooden one, in the corner opposite where he sat. He had somehow looked past it during his earlier considerations.

The second door had a knob instead of a handle. The man grabbed it and pulled, yet it held fast. There must have been tension on the door, however, because when the man grabbed it again he inadvertently gave it the barest of turns, and the door opened a crack. He pushed it completely open then, spied a short hallway going straight ahead, and a doorway without a door immediately to the right. He entered cautiously and walked down the hall.

Off the hall were three rooms, two to the left and one which it emptied into. The first was for personal services: showers and so forth, which the man couldn't comprehend. He turned a silver knob below one of the shower heads, but the only response were a few heavy drops of rusty water. The man found them rather poor tasting. In the next room were two sets of triple bunks, one to each wall left and right of the entrance. A pair of undistinguished desks were placed back to back at the far end of the room. The individual beds were crisply made with blue blankets topped by thin white pillows. In the last room the set-up was identical. Each room was lit by lights over the desks, which themselves had paper and pens stored neatly at their top right corners. The man, for lack of ability, left things alone.

He retreated to the single room to the right from where the hallway began. The left inside wall ran parallel to the hall, and was twenty feet deep. The far wall supported cabinets, both floor and wall style. A white counter was atop the floor cabinets and was interrupted by a sink. To the left with its back to the hall wall was a long earth toned upholstered couch. A square table was in the corner: it matched the height of the couch arm. Two huge overstuffed chairs sat along the back wall. Between them was a yard tall brown box, with buttons and indicators arrayed about the front. On the right wall, which ran straight in from the entrance, was a tall white metal object, with a brown false wood handle that ran the heighth of an apparent door.

The man strode to the corner table and sat himself in the adjacent chair, sinking delightfully into it. On the table were two books, hardback and without ornamentation. One was closed, the other open. He picked up the closed one and sheepishly opened it, unsure what he had. He slowly peeled the first page back, then the next, and another, until he was flitting the pages as if shuffling a deck of cards. Suddenly the man stopped, and watched as the papers settled. Two, of course, were left open. Among other things were these words:

We are told that what is threatened is "man qua man" or "man in his humanity" or "man as Thou not it" or "man as a person not a thing." These are not very helpful expressions, but they supply a clue. What is being abolished is autonomous man—the inner man, the homunculus, the possessing demon, the man defended by the literatures of freedom and dignity.

His abolition has been long overdue. Autonomous man is a devise used to explain what we cannot explain in any other way. He has been constructed from our ignorance, and as our understanding increases, the very stuff of which he is composed vanishes. Science does not dehumanize man, it de-homunculizes him, and it must do so if it is to prevent the abolition of the species. To man qua man we readily say good riddance. Only by disposing him can we turn to the real causes of human behavior. Only then can we turn from the inferred to the observed, from the miraculous to the natural, from the inaccessible to the manipulable.[*]

The man closed the book. It seemed that his playing was ended. He placed the book where it had been left. He couldn't understand all of it, as the words were of an archaic language. But he could understand enough.

---

[*]   Skinner, B. F. Beyond Freedom and Dignity, Alfred A. Knopf, New York, NY 1971, pg 190.

The sullen white-clothed figure turned to inspect the open dissertation. He took it gently into his lap, taking care to keep the same pages open. The words read thus:

The strength of such a critic lies in the words 'merely' or 'nothing but.' He sees all the facts but not the meaning. Quite truly, therefore, he claims to have seen all the facts. There is nothing else there: except the meaning. He is therefore as regards the matter at hand, in the position of an animal. You will have noticed that most dogs cannot understand pointing. You point to a bit of food on the floor: the dog instead of looking at the floor, sniffs at your finger. A finger is a finger to him, and that is all. His world is all fact and no meaning. And in a period where factual realism is dominant we shall find people deliberately inducing upon themselves this doglike mind. A man who has experienced love from within will deliberately go about to inspect it analytically from outside and regard the results of this analysis as truer than his experience. The extreme limit of this self-blinding is seen in those who, like the rest of us, have consciousness, yet go about to study the human organism as if they did not know it was conscious. As long as this deliberate refusal to understand things from above, even where such understanding is possible, continues, it is idle to talk of any final victory over materialism. The critique of every experience from below, the voluntary ignoring of meaning and concentration on fact, will always have the same plausibility. There will always be evidence, and every month fresh evidence, to show that religion is only psychological, justice only self-protection, politics only economics, love only lust, and thought itself only cerebral bio-chemistry.[*]

---

[*]   Lewis, C. S. The Weight of Glory, Harper San Francisco, Harper Collins Publishers, New York, NY, 2001, pg. 113.

With the same consideration as when he picked it up the man returned the book to the table, leaving the same pages opened.

Mankind had turned its favor on the first argument, whose rebuttal fell on deafened ears. The program crept forward, slow enough for men to accept yet fast enough to be irrevocable. The species was refined, and in a vile sense enlightened. Man had taken firm grasp of his destiny, and fell victim to a subtle Armageddon.

The man stared into space from his chair, pondering the words he had read. It was fortunate at this point that he knew no history or their tone may have had a more ominous impact. Eventually his attention wandered, to re-focus on the tall object opposite his seat. He rose and went to the refrigerator. Inside were many dark green bottles, corked rather than capped. He removed one; the liquid inside sloshed about as the man twisted his wrist. He presumed it was water. The cork was only half pushed in, so that with relatively little effort the man pulled it off the top. A sweet smell wafted to his nostrils. The man was thirsty, so he took a gulp of the stuff.

The liquid was heavy, and it burned a little going down. It was wine, a type of port to be more exact. The entity within protested heartily but the man saw fit to drink again. He guzzled the wine with far greater emphasis than he had ever drank water. The sweetness stayed in his mouth, and the burning wasn't all that bad once you were accustomed to it. He began to move around the apartment freely, taking a more scientific look at the place now that the awe of discovery had worn thin. He could get to like it easily enough.

He did in fact begin to like it very much as the alcohol took command. Not that he was rip-roaring drunk; he had not really drank that much. But as with most others who had never had alcohol before it didn't take much to have an effect. The man drew one long final swig before leaving the bottle on the table in the first room. He walked about in a controlled stagger, and kept nearly falling only to regain his balance at the last second. It was, actually, graceful, as though he intended the parody of a drunk. Somehow he managed to get around the table and leave the library. He did not need any help. And thankfully he could not sing.

The man hesitated at the entrance to the couch room. His eyes reflected the haziness of his mind, and he shook his head vigorously in an attempt to clear it. He was not successful. Sleep was coming on fast: the man's eyes were closing for an instant or two at a time in alteration. Every time they reopened, however decidedly or obliquely, the man was left with a stupefied, shocked appearance.

Then, unexpectedly, he was at the end of the counter. Before him was the box with the buttons and indicators, which he grabbed at, and in so doing hit a button with his thumb. Several lights popped on around the top facing of the object, but the man didn't notice them. He rolled himself around as he fell into the adjacent chair, and was instantly asleep.

The man awoke with the oddest feeling in his head. A dullness had taken root: not an actual pain, but close. He sat up straighter, trying to excise from his head a noise which he did not recognize. It seemed to come from everywhere. And well it should: it was music, and the male figure slowly understood it was no game of the entity's or trick of the drink at work. He now saw the lights on the box, but the instrumentation didn't seem to come from there. Hidden speakers took the sound away from the source. As he grew comfortable with the sound the man dropped his mental reservations and just sat back to listen.

The music was studious and intellectual; it was appropriate to an academic atmosphere. It was music to think by, the kind that clears your head. The man closed his eyes; the dullness faded quietly, and he allowed himself to drift. He was away for many delicious moments, pleasantly separate from the world, his thoughts sharp and crystalline even though they were unspoken. In too short a time the spell was broken. The man thought he heard a something out of the ordinary, like the shuffling of feet. He tried to regain his escape but had his attention shaken: it looked as if something moved in the front room.

The man lifted himself from his seat. The music was louder as he stood, and sounded as if it came from the room with the books. He went to the door of the room he was in, and watched. No motion was apparent. He moved his head to peer deeper into the front room only to see his bottle of port, which wasn't really on his list of favorite things just then. Slipping into the hall, the man glanced in the direction of the dimly lit bedrooms on the chance that the movement was directed their way. There was no evidence of that. He continued cautiously towards the library, entered it, and turned to the right. Half between him and the door to the cave stood a man reading.

Not a man, actually, but a specter. Yet it was so obviously harmless that the man felt nothing about it except wonder. He watched intently as it turned the pages of its equally spectral book. The apparition was an older man, with dry, thick gray and white hair combed straight back. He wore a green sweater that dropped past his hips, covering the top of his brown pants. The collar protruding from above the sweater indicated a white dress shirt underneath. The specter was clean shaven, and decidedly professorial. It turned a few more pages, deliberately and without sound.

The man considered, not without suggestion, if perhaps the image was in result of the wine. But no matter. He would inspect it at close range. Creeping forward so as not to scare the specter he saw that the older fellow was nearly his height and undoubtedly his species, yet somehow more defined in spite of his shadowy constitution. Finally the two were next to each other, although the reader took no interest in the man. The skin-and-bones reached to touch the specter, but grasped air instead.

He was dumbfounded more than anything else. He was certain someone had stood there, reading. Yet there was no longer a sign of anyone. Perhaps the wine? No; someone had been there.

Looking over to his left a few seconds later the man saw the professor standing with his back towards him. By the actions of his shoulders he must have been studying another volume. The man stared across at him, and started around the table with great forbearance, assuming he had done something wrong in his first approach. The man spread himself flush against the wall of books until he was virtually slinking along them. But the image began to fade before the man reached it, and he was left staring at nothing.

The man knotted up his face. There was no reason the other should avoid him. He wasn't angry but was confused and, truthfully, hurt. The other was so different in appearance, so odd in manner, so generally unlike anything he had ever seen. He should make an interesting acquaintance.

Then the apparition was seated at the end of the table. A large book was in front of him, not thick but wide and long. The man ventured stealthily towards him, determined to make a connection. As he edged closer to the specter the man took notice of the book. It was jammed with letters, many of them fine and ornate and overtaking whole words, words of a forgotten tongue. The man stood alongside the table and studied the text, attractive although pointless to someone who didn't know the language. Then, for no particular reason, he raised his head.

The specter was staring straight into the man's eyes: he felt as if it were seeing right through him. It was. The man's perfectly blue eyes were nonetheless shallow, with but the most ambiguous hints of rationality. There wasn't anything about them to stop a piercing glare.

In the specter's brown eyes were profound thought, emotion, and introspection. Nothing could possibly be seen beyond that. The man looked into them: he had no choice, he had been caught. Eventually he was allowed to draw back. A sadness came over the face of the apparition, a deep, wrenching sadness. It stayed that way until it had burned itself into the man's memory. He was on the verge of looking away when the ghost faded till it was gone, and the man was left staring at a frightfully empty chair.

CHAPTER THIRTEEN

It had been several days since the incident in the library and the uneasiness the man felt about it was nearly gone, although the entity tried occasionally to resurrect the insecurity. He liked the cave dwelling and was considering whether to stay there permanently. The man had also been exploring the nearby area, becoming familiar with it to the point of establishing landmarks. Downstream to where the river began to veer left was a half day from the cave. Upstream, there was a huge tree whose largest branches hung over and dipped its leaves into the water. That, too, was a half day away. Behind the cave, in the hills and woods the same distance, sat a boulder about four feet in diameter. He had not yet been across the river.

The cave was a suitable place to live. Inside the apartment the man was safe from the weather: rain had passed through his domain once already, but he was able to stay dry and move about. Food was plentiful. The berries were abundant: they never seemed to rot or fall to the ground, and no matter how many the man ate there always appeared to be the same number left on the bushes. An orchard supplied with a variety of fruit trees was over to the left from the cave mouth.

The cabinets in the kitchen were stocked with dried foods in vacuum pouches. The man had eaten a cross-section of these: the vegetables weren't very good, but he could not be expected to know about reconstitution. The meats became his favorites, although they were harder than most of the other foods and quite salty. And though he generally drank water from the river (he had discovered how to carry it to the apartment in empty food pouches) he did learn to take the wine more slowly, better appreciating it in small doses.

As the man was staying in the area to take advantage of its bounty the bounty was taking advantage of him. No longer was his face taut and lean: there was a puffiness in his cheeks, and a rounder jaw. His torso was not quite so affected, yet there was a noticeable bulge distributed across his stomach which might have been bigger if not for the constraints of his clothing. Yet he was far from being in poor health. The new types of food and drink, along with the fact he could eat at his leisure, were the reasons for his physical change. His well-being was not affected, and he wasn't concerned with how he looked anyhow.

The man was losing all concept of day and night. He generally managed to keep the two in order, sleeping at night because it was easier to see outside during the day particularly as he loved hiking through the countryside. Yet there were times that he stayed indoors for so long that the only way to know whether it was dark or light was to go outside. At times he wanted to be awake at night, to sit atop the hill and gaze at the stars. That would throw off his awareness of the time as badly as long indoor sabbaticals did.

After several weeks the man had learned that the books could be removed individually from the shelves. He loved to take them one or two at a time and browse through them, usually page by page in meticulous fashion until a given tome grew boring, at which point he'd replace it exactly where he'd found it. Each book, the developing intellect believed, had its own special place, and he wasn't about to violate the order.

Tall atlases stood on one of the corner bottom shelves: they became the man's favorites. He didn't know what they represented but was interested in the use of color and line. Most of the lines were crooked; on some pages the colors obeyed them and on others, no. It was the blue of the oceans and lakes, however, which taught him that different pictures were sometimes the same things.

Even the books which had nothing but words held the man's attention well. The ends of paragraphs and chapters broke the pages into squared and rectangular patterns as stylish in their own right as the atlases were in theirs. Chapter titles and important thoughts were often in bold or italicized print. There were the occasional huge plain letters which adorned the top corners of many pages. He had even noticed changes in the style of print between books. Most importantly, though, the books helped the man suspect a little better just who he was.

To the entity within the man this all nothing but play. It was more concerned that the longer he strayed from the proscribed path the less apt he was to return to it. The more attached he grew to his surroundings, no matter how pointless the attractions might be, the greater the chance of a permanent break with civilization. Yet no amount of cajoling worked: the man was taking root.

One morning the man ate a breakfast of berries as he tried to determine what to do that day. He was restless enough to want a challenge: indoor activity was not then particularly appealing, and hiking the nearby woods lacked promise. He knew the area too well these days, and you can't read all the time. A sense of adventure hung in the atmosphere and the man was willing to pursue it. He chose to venture upstream along the river. The visual tricks caused by walking against the current would offer a bit of entertainment.

The water happened to be running high so that the man was forced to wade through it in places. Initially he tried to avoid the wet altogether by staying among the trees near the shore, but was punished with a couple of tears on the shoulder of his garment. The outfit material had lost its strength: there were others rips in it, and stains caused by wine and food, with patches of dirt which had been permanently drilled into the fabric. His clothing wasn't quite decrepit yet, but the harm inflicted on it was more obvious every day.

Soon the river overran the bank and into the trees. The man elected to wade into the water only because he wasn't ready to turn back just then. As it was, the farther into the river he inched the more he thought it interesting to get as deep as possible. He had never been in past his ankles before.

Slowly, carefully, and with some reservation the man walked into the water. Once he retreated slightly when it felt as though the current was about to pull him down. He began to take small, purposeful steps, using the advantage of his strength to hold himself up. Keeping his feet close together at the river bottom and raising them only just enough to move helped his steadiness, too. His feet sank deep into the unseen mud. Leaning forward, he discovered, allowed him to counter the current all the better. Eventually he was in to his shoulder blades, nearly to the middle of the river. He held his arms aloft from his sides and bent forward at the elbows: this helped maintain his balance.

The man liked the heaviness of the water all around him. And it gave him a different view of the world: there was a wider panorama of the familiar side of the waterway while the unfamiliar side, being closer, was considerably more inviting. The man had only just made up his mind to visit that shore when his foot slipped and his head went under.

It was a struggle for but a moment. The man didn't shut his eyes, so that he could see the air his fall pulled down bubble back to the surface. He didn't inhale, due to fear rather than reason. The sunlight on the waves teased him, and for a second he thought how much more dazzling it was from underwater. This consideration washed away quickly as the onset of his trouble produced a greater worry: what was happening, what should he do? Instinctively he began to paddle his feet and rotate his arms. The motions brought him into the air, of which he took huge gulps.

Now the man was able to keep his head above water, but he could not control his direction. He was turned backwards, toward the cave, and the current carried him that way. He tried and failed to get a footing on the river bottom. The helplessness of his predicament weighed upon his mind, a sentience still clouded by an imperfect sense of time: no concept of death, yes, but little idea of tomorrow or even later today. It was a fear of the unfamiliar: the things he was comfortable with rarely bothered to overtly ask the questions of eternity. His prevalent thought was almost that this swim would never end, and he didn't want to think of that. The germ of a request floated into the boundaries of his thoughts: he asked to get beyond this problem. For no apparent reason his legs then rose to the surface, forcing his shoulders down. He began kicking his legs while plunging his arms end over end, and found he gained a better control of situation.

Swimming came easily to the creature. Aided by, while not fighting, the current, he was able to tread water with ease in no time. Soon he was proceeding downstream with almost no effort. He made up the area covered by his morning constitutional very quickly, passing the cave entrance almost before realizing it. The first fish in the stream in years relaxed into the stroke of a champion. The man unexpectedly found himself where the river bent left, and managed to reach the shore opposite his home ground. He studied the land intently as the water dripped from his suit.

For several seconds he stood firm before the opportunity now available dawned on him. It wasn't actually by design that the man had ended up on this side of the waterway. But, no matter: he might as well explore it while he was here. There wasn't much point in staying along the river: he knew it from walking on the far shore. Yet the entity encouraged the safety of the idea, and indeed the unknown promised nothing in particular. The man weighed his options. He would go inland, at an angle away from the cave roughly in line with the river. Certainly this was bold. But boldness hadn't cost much before as it was.

Forest travel was not simple. The trees stayed closely knotted, the underbrush was thick, and the ground was soft. Often the man couldn't even see where his feet touched the earth. Further, he couldn't keep a straight path, and his route became so skewered that he lost any sense of where the river ran. He was doing little now but rambling, which was okay. It was an increasingly greater treat to delve into the new land.

At length the man stumbled into a fairly wide clearing. It was long and narrow, with the trees forming neat lines on each side. High grasses covered the area. The man paused to look over the open field. There seemed nothing spectacular about it, so he continued across towards the forest on the other side.

The human figure covered the ground quickly, ending on a small patch of dry and sandy ground of which he took only the barest notice. Then his foot hit something, and he stumbled badly. Reaching out to catch himself the man nevertheless crashed onto the earth. He wasn't hurt, nor angry. If anything, he was surprised. The man stayed on the ground long enough for the dust to settle. He rose to determine what caused his tumble.

Backtracking, he discovered a reddish-gray ridge about four inches across. Taking a step down, for the man noticed a rise from the direction he had come, the thing was also that much tall. On the side where he had fallen was no evidence of height: the dirt was basically even to the ridge top. The ridge was not smooth. Pock marks, low spots, and gouges marred it. There was a sort of rounded corner between the top and side. The ridge, the man figured, was some type of stone. It disappeared under a cover of earth nearly ten feet away in each direction.

The man surveyed up and down the length of the stone until it occurred to him that it was in line with the row of trees on that side of the clearing. This led to his discovery that the clearing itself was very long: out of sight in both directions. So, then, rather than penetrating the woods any farther the man elected to follow the clearing along that edge. Perhaps he had found something interesting.

Or perhaps the interest was a long way off. After covering a couple miles the man considered abandoning his quest and returning to the cave—if he could find his way back, for he was no longer with any idea of where home lay. But then a second section of red-gray rock appeared, shooting from beneath a layer of soil six feet in front of him. The man presumed it was an extension of the earlier part: the same identifying marks were present.

The entity began sending messages of quite a different nature than it had ever sent before. It still implored the man towards safety, but not the safety of the prim world he had left weeks ago. That ideal was temporarily dropped in a grudging admittance he would not then pay it heed. The force within the man had to deal with him on his terms, latching onto whatever thoughts were in his framework. It had to be content with anything that might get the man out of this dangerous area, which this instant meant convincing him of the importance of getting back to the cave. It was a poor way to go, too much of a concession to the human creature. But this was developing into a bad, a very bad, situation.

Yet the man was not ready to end his romp. Open land still reached far to the front. He came across another stretch of rock, and quickly thereafter came a fourth. Suddenly he noticed something odd toward the center of the field. There was a large space with no grass, not a hint of vegetation. The man went to inspect this.

An oval of asphalt lay there, bleached gray after untold years of abuse by the sun. A series of faded and broken yellow lines were barely visible down the middle. The man was on what had once been a road; the long stones were the curb of that side. Where the soil had reclaimed the road were the grasses, while no trees had grown on the roadway proper because the dirt had not yet become deep enough for any to take firm root. The blacktop, also, was too strong and deep to be pierced from underneath: a layer of reinforced concrete was below it. The man was on a major roadway from earlier times. He knelt to the pavement and felt the rough texture. Bits of tar went to pebbles, a few of which rolled out of sight. The man deduced the patch of black wasn't natural. He determined to follow along the clearing until he could figure out what it meant.

But not just then. The sun was low in the sky, and he had learned that was a signal the day was ending. He would come back next day to continue the hunt. The problem, though, was in how to return to his apartment.

But then, for nor apparent reason, the man started straight across the field and entered the forest on the same side as he had entered the clearing hours before. The light was going fast, making the trees all the more difficult to forage through. Soon the man was grasping for anything that might help him along, grabbing at trunks and weeds and branches, angling left even though he had lost any sense of direction. Finally he heard one of the most familiar and delightful of sounds, and the woods opened onto the river.

The moon shone gaily over the water, and the man saw he was nearly directly across from his cave. By some luck he had found it; or is there any such thing as luck? The man did not know to ask the question. Simply happy to be home, he dove into the water and swam, easily beating the challenge of the current as he arrived at the other shore. He ran eagerly into the cave to await the morrow.

Chapter Fourteen

Morning arrived quickly, and the man was packing food. He hadn't disposed of the bags from the dried foods, and they were coming in handy. A dozen fruits could be stuffed into a single one, enough to last about two days. After gathering fresh fruit from the orchard the man returned to the apartment long enough for breakfast. There was no reason to eat what he had just picked with the other foodstuffs so at the ready.

Bunching up his bag of fruit by the top, the man left the cave dwelling. He marched down the slope to the river as a sense of adventure and a corollary rise of excitement accented the thought of fresh discoveries. It was the opportunity, for the first time in weeks, of finding something radically new. But even if such wasn't to be, he would at least know in greater detail the world around him. His neighborhood was expanding.

The man started to dive into the water, but hesitated. He was concerned about how the water might affect his food; he never thought that water in the form of rain had touched the fruits often, with no ill effect. But he was afraid of losing them, too. The sack may slip open in his hands, or float away. However, the calmness of the river this morning convinced the man to go on and take things as they happened. He could always return for more supplies.

Swimming was more difficult under a load, which the food certainly was as it followed the man's stroke in and out of the water behind his right arm. The bag began to slip once but he never lost it. The man made the far side with his baggage unharmed and intact. So much for that.

Next, the man felt he needed to find the place he had exited the forest the evening last, presuming it to be the quickest path back to where he'd left off. He walked downstream a few paces and saw nothing, then upstream as far with identical results. He was ready to merely guess when something told him to try a little farther against the current. This he did, and was soon at a place where the foliage was beaten down in a line heading deep into the woods. The man was confident now of his route.

It seemed to be taking far too long to get through the forest, and the man started to fear he had gone the wrong way after all. But then the clearing opened up before him, and he knew he had simply grown impatient. A sudden step down caught him off guard: there was a curb on this side just like the one on the other. He though that interesting, but went to the far ridge of the clearing to resume his journey anyway.

For a long part of the morning the trip was uneventful, the blue sky and sun overhead and the green of the forest to the side. Patches of asphalt exposed themselves at irregular intervals along with stretches of curb. The first significant development was initially inadequate to the man's desires: a thin although noticeable line traced along the horizon. The clearing was widening steadily until the man was in the middle rather than edge of it. The blue of the sky rose as the line ahead thickened and blackened. The now frail looking and greater isolated traveller was becoming ill at ease as he crept closer to what was turning into a wall of darkness. Yet his pace didn't slacken. Whatever it was, the man would inspect it.

The wall continued to grow until the horizon loomed high above the ground. As the man approached the blackness he saw it was flecked with spots of deep green. Then gnarled brown streaks came into the picture. The man realized it was a forest, but one apparently far more dense than any other. The trees were extremely tall, several hundred feet apiece, and proportionally huge at their trunks. The massive plants dwarfed the being to insignificance.

The forest looked nearly impenetrable. There were places where the trunks were only a few inches apart as high as six and seven feet above ground. An evil and uninviting darkness covered everything beyond the first row of trees. Vision couldn't have been more than fifty feet once inside the woods. The man did not like this in any way, yet he had come too far to turn back at the first adverse condition. He veered left, and at about the center of the decayed road peered high into the trees. He was awestruck to the verge of fear. He lowered his vision, and entered the forest sideways between two monoliths.

Immediately the man saw that the continuation of his trek would be part walk and part climb. It was impossible to go more than four steps without having to clamber over or around something. After several minutes the man turned, and was nearly blinded by the glare from outside the forest. His eyes had to readjust to the darkness when he turned back; as his vision settled the man realized there would be light enough for him to see where he was going, but only just enough, so that his vision wouldn't be comfortable. The forest was lit sort of like the late twilight of a cloudy day, fading quickly to black a few scant feet away from the man.

The roof of the forest was hopelessly entangled. There was no way of telling the trees apart once they were a few feet off the ground. Brown trunks narrowed into pockets of the deepest green which quickly went dark themselves. The man proceeded carefully, his feet sinking partway into the damp earth. Moisture, held in by the trees, had settled into the ground. The man could taste the dampness as he moved.

The longer he was in the forest the more comfortable he became. Soon there was no evidence of sunshine. Yet his sight improved continually, making it easier to press on. Obstructions became more readily apparent: the man could start bypass maneuvers around the more onerous ones well before reaching them. He tried to maintain the line from which had had entered these woods; he wished to go as straight as possible, to have a known exit.

Odd shapes began to appear, mostly to the sides of the explorer. Some were akin to the jagged spires of the cave but in greater numbers and more compact form, often running into one another to create intermittent ragged edges. The man could see that below the tips of the spires it was usually flat black, cutting off the view to beyond. The further distant objects sat eerily at the end of his vision. It was a benefit that the man had no preconceptions of the spookiness generally related to such ghoulish woods.

As he peered far into the trees ahead the man observed a particularly dark area exactly in his line. It was so elongated that there was no obvious way around. Above it the leaves began abruptly, in a long straight line rather than sloped gently downward. When the man was close enough he could see the thing was not black but gray, with a gridwork of horizontal and vertical lines in a staggered pattern. Rows of rectangles were offset by half to the ones immediately above and below. A powdery white substance had grown in several places. He had found a cinder block wall twelve feet high.

The man looked up the barrier, then down it in both directions. The darkness of the forest took over before he could see either end, but he saw clearly the top. Obviously he had no choice but to go over it. To the right was a tree which had grown nearly flush against the wall, touching it at the base while only a couple of feet away at the roofline. The man heaved himself up into the monster and took a sitting position with his back against the trunk and feet upon the blocks. This allowed him to walk up the wall. When he reached the top he switched his legs to the tree and grabbed the wall in his hands, hesitating to look over and beyond it.

He couldn't tell in particular what was there. The ground was brown, he thought, and murky. The area was strewn with moss covered boulders. The trees less grew out of the earth as erupted from it, as evidenced by the buildup around the lowest parts of their trunks. The man climbed atop the wall, turned and restored his grip, then lowered his body until it was stretched down the inside of the wall, and let himself drop to the ground.

He landed without a sound. His feet sank a couple inches into the muck that was the forest floor. He took a couple of steps forward, the ground pressed into itself by the force of his weight. The man was inadvertently leaving a trail, for the earth did not rise again once he had passed. Shallow footprints proceeded from two deep backward prints at the base of the wall. The man studied the lumps and boulders lying haphazardly about. They were the grown-over chunks of what had been a roof, the roof which had covered a building, the remains of such the man now contemplated. The brown muck was what was left of the floor, wood so rotten it was ponderously melting into the earth.

The man was at the outskirts of an ancient city. It had been buried deep inside a thick forest just as a few of its sisters had, in the belief it would be impossible to find. As a rule the entity within each being could steer their mount clear of them. On the chance of an error, though, a shroud was dropped over the cities when and where time did not allow their total obliteration. A menacing cover was to strike fear in the curious to keep them away on their own volition.

There was little to interest the man from where he stood. He meandered idly about the area, stumbling over the pieces of roof which would to his mind always be lumps and boulders. Where the wood still appeared firm the man took to crushing it into the ground with his feet, in deference to the male penchant for destruction. This further obscured any resemblance to flooring. He soon left the former building, crossing over the flat, hard surface of the wall opposite the one he climbed: it had long ago fell on its side.

Although he didn't realize it, the man was crossing a street whose pavement was hiding under the soil. The trees were not so large now, saplings next to their gigantic peers. On the far side of the avenue the mature plants returned in force. The man found another wall, one with an overhang. He walked along it, and in a few steps came to a glass door with the dotted remains of writing across the center. The man grasped the handle but it would not budge. He cleared a large amount of soft dirt and wet, dead leaves from the bottom edge of the door, and his next attempt to open the store was successful.

It was a structure that was basically intact. The store wasn't very large: the man could see the back wall in spite of the added darkness of the indoors. A tree had fought its way through the floor to the left of center from where he stood. The branches had not yet been able to punch through the roof, so that they bowed over and hid the ceiling as well as part of the side walls. Surprisingly there were a considerable amount of leaves, although their color was indescribable. That there were leaves at all was likely due to the growth chemicals which had been rained on the area.

The man went further into the building until he caught a movement at his right. Backtracking, he saw an image he knew to be his own. A mirror hung on the wall, larger but like the one in the shower room of the apartment. This discovery was mere happenstance; but in the man's subconscious a connection was made between those who built this structure and those who furnished the cave.

After the pause the man approached the tree. He began to walk through it, parting the branches as they came to him. He was intent on digging all the way through the bent giant. Near the back of the tree the man yanked a branch out of his eyes, to find himself staring into the face of another man.

In truth he was at eye level with a mannequin. The man glared at it, dumbfounded. The eyes of the other man didn't seem to be looking at anything: the animate man probed far into them for signs of life but found nothing except a black dot on a crystal blue ball in each socket. The blue twinkled but was obviously fake. Reaching to touch the mannequin's face, the man felt stone cold plastic. He ran his hand over the painted hair, disappointed but unsurprised that it was plastic too. The man was profoundly saddened: he thought he had found someone.

The mannequin was wearing a blue sport jacket, gray trousers, and a white shirt. This different style of clothing impressed the man, who decided to get them for himself. Yet at the slightest touch the jacket began to tear, as did the shirt and slacks. It was probably just as well. They weren't his size.

But he now knew that there were, or at least had been, others like him. There was the replica in front of him, and the memory of the woman gone so many days now. Experience was demonstrating what the status quo denied. If he was alone, and the man in fact suspected as much, he was alone by design. That would explain why so many things were kept from him, why this place was hidden in darkness. The sense of denial, first evident at the terminals, was again energized, and growing more acute. This was silently noted by the entity, who was playing an ominous waiting game.

The man stepped away, letting the leaves hide the face of the inanimate other. When he was clear of the tree he took a quick inventory of the building. There were a couple rows of metal shelving, rusting and only partially standing, to one side. A pair of doors had fallen from the dressing room entrance. A dead surveillance camera pointed inward from a corner. None of this meant anything to the man, who turned his back on it and left.

He walked around the structure to where he figured to resume his more or less straight course through the forest. Initially he encountered only more false boulders. Once he stumbled over another curb, many of which could still be found on the uneven forest floor. Later the man noticed a series of worn wooden beams pointing upward about twenty feet. It was the remains of a residential district, and the beams were what was left of the homes that once populated the land. Many of the trees used the beams for support, or had as saplings, for there were instances where a beam appeared to shoot out of the center of one. Generally the trees kept to just outside or solidly inside where the homes had stood. No walls or roofs were intact, though at random intervals a cross-beam would connect a pair of uprights. The man passed by these things for most of the middle of the day.

Beyond the residential district came a series of partially standing buildings many blocks long. Walls had fell inward or outward in helter skelter fashion over the course of the structures, and several had their roofs caved in. Gaping holes left huge maws, as though blown out by cannon shot, in some. And then it happened that more and more of the places were intact. The city's remnants became increasingly sturdy and complete the farther the dirty, white-suited creature pushed into the forest.

The man crawled into a building whose corner had found its way to the earth. Inside, firmly standing shelves were arranged in aisles; they had various forms of debris upon them. The shelves were well stocked, cans on the top ones generally, an assortment of boxes and bags on the center ones, and large decaying bags to the lowest. Many of the paper and cardboard containers were beyond rot, their contents having fallen subtly into each other to form hills of damp and matted foodstuffs laying darkly across the floor. The shelves were white metal with ample rust.

The remains on the floor were crusted over. The man was able to break off a chunk of what had been sugar, touching and sniffing it before putting it to his mouth. It tasted gristly, and he dropped it quickly as he darted his tongue about to rid it of the unpleasantness. Rice, noodles, flour, dog food and other things were spilled out, but would now be left alone.

The cans on the higher shelves offered no clue to what they held, their labels having disintegrated or been ripped away long ago. It was the ridges on them that mattered to the man once he discovered the low mettalic strum he could make by running his fingers across a can. He played for a bit, trying different cans, excited at the nuanced changes in the sounds they made. Suddenly one slipped and fell, striking his foot. Upset and maddened, the man picked it up and hurled it against a wall. It exploded at both ends before falling to the ground, leaving behind a deep red splotch. Trails began to run down the wall, making it appear to be bleeding.

The man went quickly to investigate. There were little red dots glued to the wall; they were cherries liberated from can of pie filling. The heavy juice crept ponderously downward, held back by its own thickness. The man touched it carefully, noting the sticky quality. He tasted, and was pleased to find the substance sweet.

It then occurred to him that he was surrounded by what had at least been food, though it was not necessarily worth eating by this time. At that he paused, and turned to stare into space. There were several types of food he now knew of, from this primitive stuff to the bland yet readily available food of the world he left behind. It indicated a progression: the food had been changed. So what else, perhaps, had been altered?

The question was amplified as the man took a seat on an old metal folding chair at a corner of the building. He was thinking about what had been happening to him in the last few weeks. Early memories were clouded but present, of water, of an apple, of redundant white structures. Before that was nothingness, the type as though before existence. Closer to now were clear recollections, the woman, the regal walkway, the cave home he had acquired. During it all he was changing, and had some choice in the changes. But what of the time before he was aware of himself? Who made changes in him then, and by what right?

A deep, resonant anger was rising in the man, so that he finally decided to move on rather than sit and stew. He went around to the storefront and stood for a moment. His blue eyes looked to the right and saw a line of buildings in varied states of disrepair. He walked along them, occasionally stopping to peer at their contents. One was strewn with small appliances, another with larger ones. A third offered a long counter behind which were bottles on high shelves, their contents yet present. A bookstore appeared, and the man gleefully took time to go through it. But he was disappointed to find that its volumes were in no shape for perusal.

Eventually the man arrived at an intersection. Ahead and to his right were more of the same, innumerable and disintegrating storefronts blending into the darkness of the forest. To the left, however, the woods were considerably brighter. Without much thought he turned and started down the cross street.

The brighter area grew as he neared it, and the forest was becoming a lighter shade of gray. The trees were noticeably thinner, less imposing, and farther apart. Soon the man could see the highest intensity of the brightness: centered to this was a large brown stained wooden door. The sides went straight up to about eight feet before curving inward to form a point. The door was framed in white stone which itself was set in black. A dozen stone steps led up to it.

The hesitant man went to within a few paces of the steps. He saw there were actually two doors split from the point downward with matching jet black hinges a pair to each. Large rectangular handles were alongside at the middle of the split, parallel to one another. The left door was slightly ajar.

The doors were at the corner of an impressively tall structure; perhaps too impressive. To their right, well above ground, was a gigantic window made up of many squares: much of the glass they had held was missing. The frame of the window was the same as that of the door. Below it was an aging hedge, a sparse and dying collection of bushes. At the far right was another set of doors and steps. Holding everything up was a wall of a richly charcoal colored brick.

The man turned his gaze skyward and was greeted with the sight of a monolithic tower. Just ahead of the top were twin rectangles which may have been windows; they were too high for him to tell. Over to the right a matching tower rose above those doors. Between the two was a peak, and the man caught the barest glimpse of a roof, black but illuminated, sloping in his direction.

The building forced a tremendous impact on the man. It stood as a challenge, a challenge directly to him; yet this was oddly uncomfortable. It was only a building, and he ought to be able to handle that. But the size of the thing: nothing he could recall was anywhere near as imposing among the (admittedly limited) assortment of obviously man made things he knew. He wanted to enter it but found himself without the courage. There was an ominous quality about it, about the entire immediate area, a inexplicable danger below the surface. Confusion welled inside the man uncaused by the entity within. He felt a strange mixture of fear and awe.

He crept closer to the building. The man apologetically touched the wall, rubbing it faintly, gently, trying to become more comfortable with it, acting as though he were placating an animal. The ploy was not working; the man stepped away.

He gathered himself, instinctively drawing a deep breath before climbing the stairs just enough to peek inside the door. In to the left was another door, brightly stained and standing out among the inner gloom. The man stuck his head into the opening slowly and deliberately, as if he expected it to be torn from his shoulders. That not happening, he decided to venture cautiously into the building, and grasped the right door handle. The cold rusted steel startled him.

That was all it took. He was afraid enough as it was, and had had to push himself strenuously to go as far as he did. He released the handle as he staggered backward down the steps.

From the ground the man studied the building hard, and imagined terrible things about it, things that simply weren't there. He believed there was pain; believed he would be hurt. This fear accumulated to the level of silent hysteria. The man yanked himself around to view his avenue of escape. The row of decrepit shops seemed a comfort, the darkness beyond sanctuary. In a desperately fast walk he left the monster behind.

CHAPTER FIFTEEN

The next morning the man awoke laying against a wall. He reached for his food, to find that his lunch bag was gone. In his haste the day before he had lost it. The yawning figure was disappointed yet unworried; he knew he could go without food for a short while. Pushing away from the wall, he started out of the forest. The density of the large plants caused him more trouble than before. The morning light, such as it was, was less than at other times of the day.

At the edge of the woods the man paused to look down the wall of intertwined trees. There was movement among them, a mist gently swirling from the ground to the treetops. A chill coursed through the man before he could force himself homeward.

The entity within decided it was time to speak: the man was certainly vulnerable enough. It communicated: "There is no reason to live in this manner. Existence is easier without fear. Subsistence can be provided more adequately. Time is better spent, and in greater comfort. The life left behind was superior to what is now."

The man considered the argument. There was a definite appeal: he had had enough hardship lately. Then a statement came from the man, delivered as though he and the entity were separate. "There is no recall of early life. It is not known."

"It is not important to know. It is only important to be." came the response.

As he walked along that weighed heavily on his mind. Suddenly the man blurted: "Is not 'to know' part of 'to be?'".

It was not the response the entity desired. Indeed, it wanted no response of any kind. The man had grown quick; the entity itself was subject to attack. It would remain silent for a while longer.

The man had forgotten that a perfectly obvious path through the woods would have remained available to him, courtesy of the previous trips he had made. He ended up forcing another avenue open. The going was difficult, and he was actually veering away from the cave. When he finally arrived at the river he saw by his landmark that he was far off course. Nonchalantly diving into the flowing water he swam patiently upstream and was home quickly. Catching a pole at the end of the path, he climbed ashore soberly.

He was hungry and tired and troubled, wishing to sleep but believing himself too wet to do so comfortably: his suit had lost all ability to repel water. Trodding heavily uphill, he picked berries and absently ate them. The man then walked around the orchard and ate a few of its fruits. Finally his clothes were dry, and he entered the cave seeking the comfort of his apartment.

Though he hadn't been gone long the man felt as if it had been forever. He was so entirely unsure of his surroundings in the deep forest that his greatest satisfaction now was familiarity. Quietly he toured the dwelling, thanking it for simply being there. Then it was off to the second bunk room for a rest.

The next thing the man knew he was sitting in one of the overstuffed chairs in the kitchen, looking outward. At the far end of the couch sat the woman from the picture, sideways so that she faced him. She never moved, not so much as an eyelash: she merely returned the man's stare. Yet her gaze was vacant and without register, as though she didn't really see anything.

The man rose from his seat, not taking his eyes from her. Slowly he walked towards the woman; the atmosphere tensed and grew cold and the man even felt a light draft as he saw that her eyes did not move, took no appreciation of his presence. They were drawing themselves flat. Indeed, her whole body was flattening as he began to step around it, as if pulled out from each side. When he was completely beside her it was no more than a line, bent outward where her lower back should be and downward at the knee area. He wanted to touch it but could not, his hands held back as if being held back.

He went past the stick figure, wanting now to get out of the room as an inexplicable fear refined a grip on his mindset. But that something holding him held his legs so that he fought for each step. He watched helplessly as the woman's body filled back out. A blackness was forming into her shape; when fully formed the man was made to stop and peer into it. His hand reached for it, and his fingertips slid into what was but a void. It seemed a lifetime until he could jerk his hand away, and at that with a startling violence which yanked his entire body around.

He fell onto the floor of the building with the tree inside. He lay there for a moment in a stupor before being forced up and towards the bent giant. The man fought the sensation as best he could yet was soon plowing into the monster, the tree still a tree but a beast as well, its arms sloping from the ceiling to grab him. He was pulled steadily and mercilessly through the bowels of the plant, each leaf rubbing horribly along his body, until he faced the mannequin.

Initially the two merely stood facing, inches apart. Then the mannequin grew lifelike, plastic turning to skin, hair separating to individual hairs and, most distressing, a threatening fire was rising in its eyes. The one tried frantically to get away from the transformed other, to no avail. The converted one broke out in diabolical laughter, a feat more satanic as the man had never heard laughter before. The cruel laughing went on eternally, echoing throughout the store and cutting into his body. For the moment nothing else existed.

Finally the man was allowed to turn from the cackling face, and he pressed his hands against his ears in a vain effort to escape the mocking laughter. He closed his eyes so tight the lids hurt, and when he opened them he saw only a metal framework roughly the shape of a man's head. The laughter continued unabated. The man was trapped in his place, staring at the thing, listening to the sounds until insanity threatened. Then suddenly, thankfully, he woke up.

The man remained on the bunk, breathing earnestly, for a long time before sliding off. The nightmare shook his very roots. Slowly he went to the kitchen, afraid of what might be there. Finding nothing out of the ordinary he proceeded to an overstuffed chair, his favorite, but stopped short to sit on the couch. When after a few minutes he felt no better he crossed the room and selected a dried beef packet from the cabinet. He ate in stony silence.

When he had finished the man returned to the couch. His shock was finally dying away when the entity communicated the question: "What is now kept in recall?" The terrible laughing of the mannequin immediately flared anew, rising to an insane and shrill cackle. The man fought it off with a tremendous mental effort, yet not without its having an effect. He was firmly back in a state of agitation.

"When there is recall, everything can be recalled." continued the lecture from within. "Is that what is best, to know everything? To remember pain, to re-experience terror, to wallow in agony? For each thing remembered well, another shall be remembered ill. The latter will be more enveloping."

Such a prospect appealed little to the man. But he thought of the other remembrances, those types which the entity half acknowledged, the pleasant and sweet of his journey. When he thought about them honestly enough, if he took the time to dwell among the good memories, the bad was in fact quickly overwhelmed. Soon the dream meant less. The man communicated: "Perhaps the bad will always be there. But it can be controlled."

"The effects of recall are deep and unforeseeable." retorted the entity. "Events will flow from it, sprung by unexpected forces at unexpected times. It is irrational to believe recall can be controlled."

"I just did control it." the man responded firmly.

If it were possible the entity would have been stunned. But not by the defiance: it was the use of the first person, which the man should not have been able to know. Yet there could be no doubt he was employing it or, more correctly, re-introducing it to human language. "I did control it." the man repeated, softer but actually more emphatically than before. The concept of the conscious self was born in him.

He began to play with his newfound knowledge. Rising from the couch and going to the corner he commented, "I moved here." Taking a packet of dried strawberries from a cabinet he verified, "I took those from there." The man could not know object or process names, or at least the latter not very well and the former not at all, causing a roundaboutness to his communication. Sitting back on the couch he thought "I put myself here" rather than "I have sat on the couch." Even the terms I and myself were approximations, but he definitely meant those words as they were understood in the English language of days gone by. Soon all of his expressions were in the first person.

"I will go out of this place." thought the man. He scurried to the door and opened it into the cave, acknowledging to himself what he was doing. The walk through the cave to its mouth was different than it had been, as if he hadn't ever walked it before. The lights along the way, the crags in the walls, and the finished section of the floor took on a significance, an absoluteness of being despite their inanimacy. They were; it was as though they hadn't been before then.

The outside world had also matured. The wind in the trees moved every leaf, so that a blinking tree became hundreds of motions each no less noticeable than another. Taller grasses danced gently, swaying to the rhythm of the leaves. As the man reached the foot of the hill he saw the entire picture for the first time. The berries were sewn to the side of the path, rising grandly to the cave entrance, which was stoutly protected by the ring of trees around and above it. A hint of the small orchard was available, the reds and yellows of the fruits peeking from the green which enveloped them. It occurred to the man that the place was his. He felt an inspiring sense of ownership.

Before the notion sank completely in the entity ventured to address the man. "There cannot be an I."

"There is I. I know it."

"Assume there is an I. How did the I come into being? How did the I live for all the time before the present? The I would be born of the generosity of another, which would presumably be committed to the growth of the I. The I would be provided for by that other. The I would always be dependent. It could not have come about on its own, or keep itself by its own power. Therefore, the I could not truly exist."

This line of argument troubled the man. He of course had no idea how he had come into being, knowing merely that he somehow happened to be. During what might be termed the Dark Ages of his life, the time in which he must have existed but was not aware of it, he had to have been dependent on something, and it made sense that such a thing would be good. Why else had his needs been met? Perhaps he was acting rash; there would be an obligation to a supporting force, if such a force existed. The man took time to consider the point.

Contemplation caused the man to roam about incoherently, and he eventually approached the orchard. As he entered it a question formed in his mind: "If the force the I depended on was good, why could the I not know it?"

There was no response.

The man strode purposefully down a row of the orchard. At its end he wheeled around as if to address the trees, and abruptly proclaimed "The I is beyond dependence. I can act for myself." To the man's mind, once the life he could remember began he was independent.

"No. The I is always dependent." The entity within was quite sure of the point. "Even if direct dependence is gone, there is still indirect dependence. The I still rose from it knew not what."

The man indignantly snapped, "That is wrong. There would be no dependence." He stomped towards an apple tree, ripped a fruit from it, and angrily chomped into it.

And he realized he was indeed dependent.

A rush of events surged to the front of the man's mind. It demonstrated to him a fantastic streak of good fortune: food, the cave shelter, the guidance through the woods when he was unsure of his direction. All of it was a gift: the man, on consideration, could not accept they were simply happy accidents. There were too many of them too conveniently.

He froze, perplexed. He did not like the the idea of an obligation to a power which would not allow itself to be known. Yet what else was there? Could there be some other force?

Some other force. The concept grew like the grass. An honest force, not in fear of being known, maybe wanting to be known, always willing to help its creatures along. This honesty of the other force—the man was gaining the sense to see it was extant—was the most enthralling thing about it. Even though he was hurt by them the man was not kept from the thorns of the rosebush. The wine made him feel odd but was not denied. The dark forest, of all places, was his to explore. On reflection the creature could see this other force coming through even under the controls of Man, in the canals and cultivated areas.

The man accepted his dependency. His allegiance would be to the newly discovered force, the one which allowed him freedom. He experienced Joy for the first time as he stated his pledge in the solemn language of the soul.

The other power knew now it had lost him, irrevocably, absolutely, without reservation. There was but one thing left to do and the entity, as much as it could be said to, willed it to happen. Deep in the man's body, hidden in the metabolism above whatever other potions were stored, a chemical was released into the man's bloodstream. There was nothing left to wait for but Time.

CHAPTER SIXTEEN

The man awoke the next day in the discomfort of a headache. It was initially dull but intensified gradually during the morning. He suffered one razor-thin slice of pain which was greater than any other hurt, running through his head just above the eyes and ears. Emanating from it was a throbbing that ripped steadily across his forehead and temples. The battle to fight the pain was constant and without real success. Force of will did little; only when he applied pressure to his temples would the aching subside, and even then just for a few scant and precious seconds. The man pressed his hands to his head often for just some such relief. Turning his head didn't help at any rate. Generally, it merely left him hurting worse.

He had been sitting in his chair but left it to walk around. Initially the movement helped, and a false hope that the pain would stop tortured the man in the way only lies can. Quickly the untruth exposed itself, and each step became worse than the previous. He stumbled to a bedroom, and dozed as best he could; the throbbing refused him a comfortable nap. Every time he dropped off he would soon awaken in greater pain, until he felt as though it hurt worse when his eyes were closed.

Yet another problem was brewing in the man's stomach. It was churning fiercely. He concluded it was just hunger, and forced himself out of bed and into the kitchen. Nothing of the available food was appealing. In the end he grabbed a couple packets randomly and ate the worst meal of his life. His throat tried to reject the nourishment independent of his will. After a bitter campaign the ordeal was past. The man considered a gulp of wine but took none. It was simply out of the question.

It was a pitiful figure which sat itself on the couch, determining not to move. The headache had grown intense enough that the man was squinting his eyes, which became distressed because of the squinting. His body was numbing, and actually beginning to ache too; perhaps he should move after all. Heading outside might actually help the trick to work.

Getting off the couch was an event in itself: the man's legs were asleep and unwilling to obey the orders of his brain. But with a mighty heave he was up and shuffling along, much to the displeasure of his head, which would have been content to stay indoors and immobile. Knots and corkscrews ran in masochistic glee up and down the man's legs. They were as uncomfortable as also painful. Often the legs simply refused to hold his weight, sending the frightened being remorselessly into the cave walls.

Finally he was outside: his stomach only churned more intensely, as though it of its own accord rejected the sunlight and all that came with daytime. The man elected to head for the orchard and there grabbed a pear, believing he needed to eat. One bite told him hunger wasn't the problem. The flavor of the pear instigated a chain reaction which caused the man to think his stomach was trying to work its way out of his body. Running, to his own momentary amazement, to the end of the orchard, he made it beyond the last tree before the upheaval within him came forth. He vomited all that he had eaten. Shocked and disgusted he jerked backwards, his head swimming and his body trembling noticeably. The man dropped hard onto the ground.

The man was scared, pitifully, childishly frightened. Aside from hunger his body had always been stable. His alarm heightened as a second surge rose, which he was able to fight off with a valiant effort. Yet it left the question of whether he would vomit again, whether he may be forever plagued with the awful threat.

This new fear was the most genuine the man had ever known. It was not at all like the animal panic he had felt in the rain weeks ago. Everything was blanked out then; he was too well aware of the events now around him. A third surge gathered itself and was unstoppable. The man was left standing confused in the light brush after the attack.

Eventually he was able to pull himself together enough to return to the apartment. There seemed no point to staying outside, and he was taking a chill. Knowing it would be warmer inside, and that he could throw a blanket over himself if he wanted, the apartment was the place to be. During the return, possibly aided by the dampness in the unfinished section of the cave, the chill worsened.

The man sat on an overstuffed chair. Just as felt he was relaxing he was victimized by the dry heaves, which was worse psychologically than outright vomiting. It was the strange sounds coming from deep inside his body: they echoed in his mind with greater ferocity than as they actually occurred. When the heaves mercifully subsided he got a blanket, wrapping it over his shoulders like a shawl. The increasing chill sent shivers coursing through his body; it was becoming a coldness. The man began to walk about, but dizziness was overcoming him and his legs were weakening steadily. He took another blanket, and laid on a bunk.

Shivers became shakes which evolved into convulsions. His fingers twitched, as did his feet and sometimes his head. Occasionally the man's arms, legs, or torso would jerk violently and uncontrollably. In spite of two blankets he grew colder. Sleep was foreign: he was to experience the whole process without reserve.

Soon the man's breathing became erratic. He fought to inhale deeply, forcing modest control over his lungs; yet he wasn't really doing well at it. Although he was taking in less and less air he still managed to breathe noiselessly: he never gasped, never choked, never fell to rasping. Finally he was overwhelmed and went unconscious. His body lay immobile except for the odd, barely discernible twitch.

Even in his coma the man battled so much as he could. He felt strange pain in spite of his circumstance: the man knew he was not awake, yet he felt conscious. He seemed in a void, and his body was not visible to him. The pains were a kind of pulling sensation. The man, not entirely realizing what he was doing or why he was doing it, pulled against them.

Death was no concern to him, for he still knew nothing of it. What he knew was that he liked the world he had been in and wanted to be there. He was somehow struggling to stay; he had only just arrived. And he feared wherever it was that he was.

But then, suddenly, all fear was gone. So too was the pulling. All was still and quiet; calmness was about his being. There were no colors, no evidence of a physical reality, only his self. But no. Gradually it dawned on the man that another presence was near; from it emanated the calm. He became at ease, and full of confidence that all was well. He was allowed to dwell in the presence for what seemed a blissful eternity, yet was merely less than an instant. The experience was indescribably pleasant, and the delighted creature grew more aware of who he was, more fully positive that he existed.

Far too quickly he knew it was time to leave. The man felt sorrow at the realization but was willfully resigned to his fate. The pains began again, but the pulling was in another direction now. He saw nothing yet, knowing only sensations. When these stopped he became unaware of things.

When the man awoke the illness was still upon him, at no significantly less intensity. He twitched and shivered, breathed somewhat erratically, and was yet cold. Working the blankets more tightly around his neck, the man resolved to wait the time out in bed.

He had been away for two days. Outside, the sun shown majestically across the area; inside, the minutes dragged. The man began to want to rise, but found he lacked the energy; wanted to sleep, but couldn't quite. Intense pain sporadically rolled through his body, keeping his mind on edge. He tried often to look around, but his headache, ever present, made that uncomfortable and kept his eyes nearly closed. The silence of the apartment echoed his misery. Yet thankfully, although it was several hours, he did drift to sleep.

It was not a completely restful sleep, as spasms humbled his body throughout. During the harsher ones he was momentarily awakened. His overall comeback was not affected, however, and his slumber was gratifying if nonetheless rough.Steadily his condition was improving: his breathing levelled, the quakes gradually settled, his body grew warmer.

The renewed warmth meant the most to the man, and he was happy that that precipitated the removal of part of his coverings. He lay quietly after his rest, gaining strength, until hunger, a real, demanding hunger, forced him from bed. This was an effort: his joints complained and his muscles resisted the attempt to sit up. The walk to the kitchen was tentative and quivery, yet it did drive some stiffness and soreness off. He had to lean on the counter to help himself stand.

It was then that he realized the full extent of his hunger. He grabbed the first packet in sight and ripped it apart ferociously. A second, then a third and fourth packet found the countertop. The man felt better after each serving: barbequed beef wasn't just for breakfast anymore. He uncorked a bottle of wine and took a couple of sips: its sweetness and refreshment were welcomed heartily. When he was through eating the man sat on the couch in satisfaction.

He had beaten it, whatever it was. And though he wasn't near full health the man was confident of its return. The fullness of his belly said as much, as did the warmth of his body and the calm in his mind. He nearly smiled as he laid back for a more fitful rest. And some as yet small part of him said thanks.

CHAPTER SEVENTEEN

Many uneventful weeks passed after the man had fought off his illness. He thought less about it as the time went by. He was happy living in and around the cave, taking delight in life's little pleasures, becoming more aware of his freedom day by day. Freedom led him to a patch of white wildflowers, a few of which were on the kitchen counter. It caused nighttime sabbaticals along the riverbank and in the forest, for the sheer joy of the nocturnal world. It allowed him to dwell on his existence and experience; true contemplation was no longer impossible.

The apartment itself took on a greater good. The man was learning to fully enjoy his environ, from the comfort of a chair to the look of a faux wood finish on a shelf or cabinet. Most of all, there were the books—his books. He would never be able to read them in complete understanding yet he adored them anyway, particularly the ones with photographs and diagrams that he always managed to find. Learning was possible even for a being who could not decipher all of an ancient language. The man noticed the evidence of different climates as he came across photos of snow or desert. And animals: it was obvious by their appearance they had been living creatures. Through pictures of stadiums and meetings and shopping malls he learned there had been more people like himself. He regularly closed his eyes and tried to imagine milling about with others, but the results were vague and unsatisfying. Yet they were still nice thoughts.

One day the man was sitting on the hillside milling over a large book. It was opened to an aerial view of a city, and he was studying it keenly. Squares and rectangles were formed on the ground by the gridwork of streets, and within the shapes were many buildings of various size and style. The man ran his gaze constantly along the lines of buildings before suddenly pausing and raising his sight. He stared across the river, and thought of what was beyond there. It was time to go back.

The next morning the trek began. The paths which the man had made through the woods weeks ago had long since filled themselves in, but he remembered enough to forage straight ahead; the roadway would appear at some point. As it was, the underbrush opened onto it quicker than he expected. Making a left as memory informed him, the man walked at a relaxed pace. Remembrances of the dankness and darkness of the place rolled into the front of his mind, causing a flow of second and third thoughts about the return trip. Soon the black line rose on the horizon, developing into a thick and wide monolith seemingly taller and more ominous than before. The white figure steadily slowed its approach yet continued until it was upon the wall of darkness. The veil of mist clutched the man just before he plunged into the trees.

A long time passed until the first objects appeared, a series of decaying buildings similar to what the man had seen earlier. He wandered about them for a bit just to satisfy his curiosity. The line of structures came to an abrupt end, leaving the creature to weave through the next group of trees. They were larger than most of the others, having grown in what had been a park. They were bigger because there had been no objects to slow their growth.

The man groped through the huge vegetation, steadily making some kind of progress. Whenever his feet could find ground they would sink into a layer of damp leaves, and with every step his feet grew colder. He was trying to keep a straight line but it was not possible. He was subtly veering to the right.

A patch of lighter gray at a sharp angle from him caught the being's attention. He adjusted his course to intercept it. The going was rough but the man pressed on, each forward glance telling him he was closing in on the lightness. The forest became steadily brighter as wispy grays turned into an honest light. Then the man was at the back of a structure which was standing in almost unrestricted sunlight. He knew what it was.

Still, he took a moment to study the place. Gray but darkening brick emanated from the building to form a semi-circle addition which was adorned with several narrow windows of softly colored glass. It was obviously not part of the original structure, for it wasn't as tall or wide as the rest and had a separate black roof rising to a point below the top of the entirety. At the very back of it stood a white stone, grayed over the years so that the markings were obscured, and the remains of a wrought iron fence were strewn near it. Ignoring the stone, the man began to fight through the small leaved bushes which grew right up against the addition, until he was smack up alongside the building. On the side of the main body of the building ran windows even taller than those at the back, and the wall disappeared into trees and brush. The man threaded his way steadily through the growth until he rounded a corner and went up a set of steps to a slightly opened door.

Without hesitation he tried to squeeze through but could not. Grabbing the door with both hands and summoning strength for the pull, the man gradually increased pressure until the object began to move. The savage creaking of the hinges proved traumatic, so that he ended his pull the instant the door was open enough to step through. The immediate inside looked to be a long corridor running across the front of the building. It was dark but not much that he couldn't see. Three double doorways stood closed but, the man assumed, they led further into the place. A single door at a right angle to the double doors stood closed at the far end of the hall, and another single door to his left, the one the man had seen on his first visit. He crept to that one solely on account of its proximity.

To his surprise the door opened easily and noiselessly. It led into a small room which offered nothing save a stairway against the far wall. It was brighter in the room, thanks to a window above the stairs. The man decided to climb them. They turned and emptied onto a landing where there was another door; the stairs continued to the side. He continued heading up.

The stairway wound around the walls for several complete turns. The light dimmed to the point where the man thought he might have to go back down, when he saw an opening. Entering it, he found a room with just enough light for him to see, and that only after his eyes adjusted. To the left a ladder angled upwards, and he climbed it. It appeared to end into a ceiling, which the man pressed against with his hands to discover it gave a little. Pushing upon it hard, he was treated to bright sunlight. With a mighty shove the trapdoor flew open, and the man stepped onto the roof of a squared tower.

The now brightly white frocked being stepped to the center of it and turned slowly in all directions. There was nothing nearby except green treetops at a uniform height, an emerald carpet laid out flat yet shimmering and swaying for miles around. Looking into the distance the man noted the faded blue mountains which formed the backdrop of the scene. Stepping to the front of the tower, he looked down. He was impressed by the height but it caused him to waver; he had to jump back for fear of falling over.

The man stood and marvelled at the landscape for a very long time. White spots made themselves known on the far mountains, and he wondered if they were related to the buildings he had left behind in his old life. It seemed as though he could walk across the treetops to reach them. But not that he wanted to.

Eventually the man elected to leave the roof, yet not without a final observation. He went over to a corner and peered hard into the distance.

A hill seemed to rise alone although it was among many siblings. Part of the way up it was a darkened patch, visible only because it had been sought. The corners of the man's mouth curled at the sight of his home.

He went back downstairs and into the hall. The first set of double doors opened with a heave and a squeal, and the man was quickly past. The interior loomed large; he was in awe of its size. On the ceiling were faded lines and images which appeared to be vaguely human. Similar etchings were on the windows, yet he could make out nothing precisely. The place was virtually empty, a couple of failing chairs set unevenly along the walls being the only furnishings. Marks were left on the floor in a regular pattern, but for the man they were meaningless. He went to the middle of the massive room, slowly, almost stupidly, scanning it as he moved.

It was there that he noticed a tiny red object suspended from the ceiling at the far end of the chamber. Without any real thought the man began heading towards it. As he drew closer there was an appearance of flickering to the object, not unlike the nighttime lights but more pronounced, as a candle. A tiny light danced inside of a red holder, a light which became more vivid the longer the man stared into it. He walked up to just in front of it and sat on the floor. As he sat he fell to wonder, and the wonder became thought. Then a smile spread across the face of the man while life came into his eyes.

And the light, which had burned always, would burn forevermore.

About the Author

Charles Martin Cosgriff lives in Michigan with his wife and three children. He has written freelance for many years, edited a journal of conservative views, and has been heard on local radio delivering political commentary.

0-595-20304-3

Made in the USA
Middletown, DE
01 May 2023

29816773R00092